WE'LL ALWAYS HAVE PARIS

A MARY BROWN BOOK

BERNICE BLOOM

DEAR READER

Bonjour,

Welcome to a Parisian adventure starring Mary Brown and her mother, Rosie.

In this story, the intrepid duo head to Paris for a few days to celebrate Rosie's 60th birthday. It promises to be such fun: They will shop til they drop, enjoy spa treatments, and come back as gorgeous and well-groomed as the Parisian women.

But. this is not just a birthday celebration. Unbeknownst to Mary, Rosie has planned the trip because she has something important that she must reveal to her daughter.

Through the days in Paris, Mary stumbles into a whirlwind of family bombshells and outrageous adventures that will redefine everything she thought she knew.

Along the way, there is much for everyone to enjoy. Like:

DEAR READER

- Leading a "Save the Badger" parade down the Champs-Élysées
- Fleeing the Louvre after stumbling upon a hidden government secret
- Befriending a troupe of mischievous mime artists
- Dancing the night away with Madame Macron

Mary navigates a Paris straight out of a fever dream. But amidst the chaos, the City of Love has one final surprise because Mary has a secret of her own that she is dying to share.

"Hilarious, heartwarming, and utterly unpredictable, "We'll Always Have Paris" proves that family bonds can withstand anything – even the wildest weekend in the most romantic city on Earth."

I hope you enjoy the rollercoaster x

CHAPTER 1: MARY & ROSIE

The early morning sunlight streamed through the kitchen window, casting a warm glow on Mary's face as she danced around the room, her bare feet padding softly on the cool tiles. The aroma of freshly brewed coffee filled the air, mingling with the sweet scent of the jasmine blooming outside.

'Return to sender. Do-de-do-de-do. Address on note. Do-de-do-de-do. No such number Do-de-do-de-do. No such soap,' Mary belted out, her voice a mix of enthusiasm and off-key notes.

Ted winced, the cacophony grating on his early morning nerves. He ran a hand through his dishevelled hair, fighting the urge to cover his ears. 'For the love of God, Mary. If you're going to sing at top volume in the mornings, at least get the words right.'

Mary spun around, her eyes sparkling with mischief. 'They are right.'

'No such soap?' Ted's eyebrow arched sceptically.

'Yes. Well, what is it then?'

Ted stood for a while, his brow furrowed in concentration. Slowly, he realised he had no idea, and took milk out of the fridge. 'Do you want a coffee?'

'Yes, please,' Mary replied, her feet still moving to an inaudible rhythm. 'Do you think I should go onto Britain's Got Talent with my singing?'

Ted smiled at his delusional wife, a wave of affection washing over him. He wisely resisted the urge to tell her that she sounded like nothing so much as an animal in the death throes of life. Instead, he focused on the way the sunlight caught her hair, turning it to spun gold.

'Aren't you working this morning?' he asked, reaching for the mugs, the ceramic cool against his fingers.

'Nope. I'm on afternoons. I told you.'

A mischievous glint appeared in Ted's eyes as he abandoned the coffee preparations. 'So, you're free right now for a little lie-down dancing?'

Mary's laughter, rich and full, filled the kitchen. 'You're weird.'

'I'm not the one dancing around the kitchen in my knickers and a Mickey Mouse t-shirt.'

'That's not weird at all,' Mary retorted, twirling again, the oversized t-shirt swirling around her thighs. 'Anyway, what makes you think I'm wearing knickers?'

Ted's breath caught in his throat, his heart suddenly racing. 'Oooo... don't say that. As it happens, I think you'd look much better if you jiggled around without this horrible t-shirt on,' he said, gently tugging at the hem of his wife's top.

The cotton was soft under his fingers as he slowly lifted it, revealing inch by tantalising inch of Mary's skin. She raised her arms obligingly, her eyes locked on his, a silent invitation in their depths.

'Oh wow. You were right. No knickers,' Ted breathed, his voice husky with desire.

'Bed?' Mary suggested, her skin tingling with anticipation.

'Bed,' Ted confirmed, all thoughts of coffee forgotten.

MEANWHILE, across town, the mood in another household couldn't have been more different. The Brown residence stood silent and sombre.

Rosie and Derek Brown had just endured their fourth argument of the day, each heated exchange leaving them more drained and distant than the last. Things had become so fraught that the fighting had stopped, and an air of silence now settled over the house. It was worse than the arguing, this oppressive quiet that seemed to suck the very life from the rooms.

Rosie Brown was upstairs, keeping out of the way. She sat on the edge of the bed, her fingers tracing the familiar pattern of the quilt she'd made years ago when things were happier. Each stitch held a memory, and now they seemed to mock her with reminders of what she was losing.

She picked up the phone to call someone…anyone…she just needed to vent. In the end, she opted for Pauline, her lovely friend from the bridge club. Rosie, Pauline and Katherine had become best of friends since they all started heading to the club twice a week, they knew each other inside out and back-to-front. Pauline answered and Rosie burst into tears.

Downstairs, Derek was in the living room, sipping his coffee. The bitter taste matched his mood as he flicked absently through the day's news. He regarded each story dismissively, with a weariness borne of disappointment with himself. The rustle of the newspaper pages seemed unnaturally loud in the quiet house.

Mortgages were due to rise again, the doctors were on

strike again, and more kids were playing truant than ever before. What a joy. Just what he needed when his world was falling apart. The weight of their crumbling marriage pressed down on him, making even the act of reading the paper feel like an insurmountable task.

Then, when he thought things couldn't get any worse, the silence abated, and the sound of crashing and bashing came thundering through the ceiling. His wife appeared to be rearranging all the furniture upstairs, each thud and bang a physical manifestation of her inner turmoil.

'Is everything okay?' he shouted, without leaving the huge armchair that he'd come to think of as 'his'. When he and Rosie went their separate ways, he was taking it with him. She'd have to stop him if she didn't want him to. It was a childish thought, but it gave him a small sense of control in a situation that was rapidly spiralling beyond his grasp.

'Rosie,' he tried again, his voice echoing in the space between them. 'Is everything okay?'

Rosie's response came back sharp and bitter. 'What do you think? Do you think everything's OK?'

Derek sighed, the weight of their failing relationship pressing down on his chest. 'Come downstairs, and let's talk about it.'

'I'm done talking,' Rosie shot back, her voice thick with unshed tears. 'I never want to talk to you again.'

Derek picked up the paper but couldn't concentrate on anything. The words swam before his eyes, meaningless in the face of his crisis.

'I'm going for a walk,' he shouted to his wife before grabbing his coat and heading for the door. The fabric was cool under his fingers, contrasting the heated, oppressive atmosphere in the house.

'Great, just leave. That will sort everything out,' Rosie's voice dripped with sarcasm as she came onto the landing, her arms full of clothes. 'Always best to leave when things get tough, isn't it, dear?'

Derek felt a surge of frustration rise within him. 'Oh, don't be so dramatic. I'm going for a walk. Isn't that what the doctor said? He told me to do more exercise. He said the pre-diabetes and blood pressure will benefit from a healthier lifestyle. Why do you always have to make out that I'm the bad guy? For God's sake, I'M JUST GOING FOR A WALK.'

The door slammed behind him, the sound reverberating through the house like a gunshot. Rosie Brown burst into tears. The clothes fell from her arms as she sank to her knees on the landing. The sobs wracked her body, pouring out years of unspoken hurt and disappointment in a torrent of emotion.

Outside, Derek stood on the doorstep, his hand still on the doorknob. The cool air caressed his face. He could hear Rosie's muffled cries through the door, and for a moment, he was tempted to go back in, to try and make things right. But the chasm between them seemed too wide, too deep to bridge with mere words.

With a heavy heart, he stepped off the porch and began to walk, each step taking him further from the house but not from the problems that awaited his return. The neighbourhood around him bustled with life – children laughing, dogs barking, the distant hum of lawnmowers – all oblivious to the quiet tragedy unfolding behind the Browns' front door.

As Derek walked, his mind raced with thoughts of what had brought them to this point. How had they gone from the young, carefree couple who'd fallen in love to these strangers living under the same roof? The weight of unspoken words and unfulfilled dreams hung heavy on his shoulders.

Back in the house, Rosie slowly gathered herself, wiping away tears with trembling hands.

CHAPTER 2: PARISIAN DREAMS

It was considerably later that day, when the warring parents had settled down and dared to be in the same room as one another, that they began to talk. Once a place of comfort and family gatherings, the living room now felt like a battleground. The air was thick with tension.

Derek cleared his throat, the sound unnaturally loud in the quiet room. 'There isn't any need for this to get nasty. We can deal with it sensibly and maturely. There's no need for drama.'

Rosie's bitter laugh cut through the air like a knife. 'Sure. Easy for you to say. The easiest way for us to avoid drama and be sensible and mature would be if you didn't want to end our marriage.'

Derek sighed, running a hand through his thinning hair. 'It's not that I'm ending our marriage. Here you are - getting all dramatic again.'

'Yes, it is, Derek,' Rosie snapped, her eyes flashing with hurt and anger. 'It's exactly that you're ending our marriage. That's what you're doing.'

'The last thing I want to do is hurt you,' Derek said softly, his words hanging heavily between them.

Rosie's shoulders sagged, the fight draining out of her. 'Yep, and that's what everyone says when they hurt someone.'

Derek leaned forward, his elbows on his knees. 'OK. Look, I can't win here. I don't feel like this is my doing. I feel like we've grown apart. Can you honestly say that you're happy with the way things are? Can you?'

The silence stretched between them, filled with years of unspoken disappointments and unfulfilled dreams.

'No,' Rosie finally admitted, her voice barely above a whisper. 'I thought we might work on it, that's all.'

'I'm sorry,' Derek said, the words feeling inadequate even as he spoke them.

'So you said.'

'I am, though. I'm so sorry, but we haven't been happy for ages. Not happy like we used to be. We'd both live more fulfilling lives if we weren't together.'

Rosie shook her head, a wry smile twisting her lips. 'There's no point in all this. We're going over old ground. You've said all this stuff before. I don't know why you think we'd be happier if we split. It's such an odd thing to do at our age.'

'We could have another 25 years. We're only 60. We've got long lives ahead of us - too long to spend in a marriage that doesn't make either of us happy.'

'I'm only 59,' Rosie said bluntly. She had no idea why she felt the need to bring that up, but right now, she'd do anything to correct and belittle him.

'Well, there we go then. You're a youngster.'

'Not exactly.'

Rosie was 60 in a few weeks. It felt like a knife through her heart that he hadn't remembered. In their 30 years together, he'd never forgotten a birthday or an anniversary.

Until now. This year he hadn't mentioned it once. The realisation brought a fresh wave of pain, threatening to overwhelm her.

'I might go away for a while,' said Rosie, her voice thick with unshed tears.

'Really? Where?'

'Somewhere glamorous to take my mind off all this.'

'Sure.'

'I might go away for my 60th. It's a week on Monday.'

Derek looked up, his face a mask of shock and guilt. The room seemed to grow colder as the implications of his forgetfulness sank in.

'I knew you hadn't remembered.'

'I had. I just…'

'Just what?'

Derek shook his head, words failing him.

'Even though I organised a huge surprise party for you, you didn't even remember my birthday. Great.'

'Look, I'm sorry.'

'So you keep saying.'

The conversation trailed off, leaving them both drained and more distant than ever. The ticking of the clock on the mantel seemed to grow louder, marking the passage of time in a marriage that was rapidly running out of it.

Across town, Mary was busy working at the garden centre, watering plants that had no need for water and rearranging gardening ornaments on a long wooden shelf for no discernible reason. The summer heat pressed down on her, making her long for the cool comfort of home.

When her phone flashed with her mother's number, she was thrilled to have a distraction. Ducking behind a display of garden ornaments, she answered the call.

'What's up, mumsy?'

'Oh, nothing much. Just pottering…sorting things out at home.' Rosie's voice sounded strained, even through the phone.

'You don't sound very happy, mum.'

'Neither do you, love,' said Rosie, defensively.

'No, but that's because I'm at work and hiding behind all the garden ornaments so Keith doesn't see me. We're not supposed to take personal calls in the shop.'

'Oh, I'll be quick then.'

'There's no need. I'm behind three rather jaunty wooden ducks in red wellies, a rustic bird bath and a gnome with a fishing rod. No one can see me.'

'Good. I was just calling to ask whether you fancied coming away with me next weekend?'

'For your 60th?'

'Yes. You remembered.' Rosie's voice cracked slightly, betraying her emotion.

'Of course I remembered, Mum. You nutcase.'

Her mum sounded close to tears, and Mary felt a pang of concern.

'Are you OK, mum?'

'Yes. I'm just touched that you remembered. So - you and me - next weekend. Or maybe head out there on Wednesday if you can get the time off, and we can have a lovely break.'

'Isn't Dad coming?'

There was a pause on the other end of the line, heavy with unspoken words.

'No, he won't come, he'll stay home. He's not been very well.'

Mary's stomach clenched with worry. 'What do you mean, not very well?'

'Nothing to worry about, love. He's fine. The doctors have told him not to travel.'

'Not to travel? Well, he can't be fine then, can he? If they're not letting him travel, something must be seriously wrong with him.'

'No, sweetheart, there's nothing wrong with him.'

Rosie was beginning to regret using a medical excuse to explain her husband's absence, but she wasn't ready to tell her daughter the truth. Not yet.

'Well, he should be able to travel, okay, shouldn't he?'

'He's not well, but it's nothing serious. They just want to do some tests.'

'OK,' said Mary, entirely unconvinced. She ended the call feeling more worried than before, a sense of unease settling in her stomach.

When she returned from work that evening, the scent of soil and flowers clinging to her clothes, she rushed to find Ted, her earlier conversation with her mother weighing heavily on her mind.

'You saw my Mum and Dad at the weekend, didn't you?'

Ted looked up from his book, sensing the concern in Mary's voice. 'Yes, why?'

'Do you think Dad seemed okay? Was he ill?'

'He seemed fine to me. Why do you ask?'

Mary sank onto the couch beside him, her brow furrowed with worry. 'Because Mum has just invited me to Paris to celebrate her 60th, but Dad can't come because the doctors have told him not to leave the country.'

Ted's eyebrows shot up in surprise. 'The doctors have told him not to leave the country? Are you sure? Isn't it usually the police and court judges who stop you doing that? Perhaps he's being pursued by the police for being involved in the great train robbery or something.'

'I'm being serious, Ted; I'm worried about him. He's 60, and the doctors have told him he's too ill to travel abroad. Don't you think that sounds serious?'

Ted's face softened as he saw the concern in Mary's eyes. He pulled her close, wrapping an arm around her shoulders. 'I'm sorry, sweetheart, of course it's serious. Do you want me to give him a call? See whether I can have a manly chat with him?'

'There's no point. You know what Dad is like? He probably won't say anything.'

'I've invited Mary to Paris next weekend,' Rosie said, breaking the silence.

'Oh, you have? That will be nice.' Derek's voice was flat, devoid of any real enthusiasm.

'Yes, it will. I told her you couldn't come, and she was very worried.'

Derek's head snapped up, his eyes narrowing. 'Did you tell her that we're separating?'

'No, of course I didn't.'

'What was she worried about then.'

Rosie shifted uncomfortably in her seat. 'I told her you couldn't come because you were ill, and the doctor told you not to travel.'

'Why the hell did you say that?' Derek's voice rose, frustration evident in every word.

'What did you want me to say?'

'I don't know - you could have said it was a girls' trip.'

Rosie shrugged. She was secretly pleased that she'd annoyed him. Every small victory helped her to cope.

'Was Ted there when you spoke to her?'

'No, I called her at work.'

Derek sighed heavily, the weight of their deception pressing down on him. 'You've made things very complicated, Rosie.'

'Nope, Derek. You've made things very complicated.'

Derek ignored the barbed comment, too tired to argue further.

'What will you do when you get there?'

'I'll go to a wonderful spa and go out for my birthday on Monday. Or we'll go and buy some designer clothes or something - I'm not sure, but it will be expensive.'

'I wouldn't expect anything less,' Derek muttered. Then, more seriously, 'Are you going to tell Mary while you're out there? She must know we're splitting up.'

Rosie's voice was bitter as she replied, 'Of course I will, Derek. I'll do all the difficult, uncomfortable and complicated things, and you just stay here in your favourite armchair.'

And so the trip was planned: a summertime adventure to the city of romance for one warring parent and a confused daughter. Mr Brown hoped that his wife would come around to the idea of them separating while she enjoyed time with her daughter under the city's bright lights. Rosie wanted to tell her daughter the news in the best way possible but had no idea how to go about it.

What neither of them realised was that Mary had a great secret of her own to impart.

It promised to be quite a trip: one that would change their lives forever.

CHAPTER 3: THE JOURNEY BEGINS

WEDNESDAY:

Mary shuffled as she tried to get comfortable. The Eurostar seats were so tiny that her large derriere spread over two of them, and the small gap between them dug into her right cheek.

'Are you OK, love?'

'Yes. Why do you ask that?'

'Well, you're doing a lot of wriggling and making a range of pained expressions.'

'We have a large bottom; small seat situation going on here,' explained Mary. 'These seats aren't big enough for a hamster's bottom.'

'Oh, I thought they were quite comfortable.'

'Yeah, well, that will be because your bottom is no bigger than a hamster's. Now, are you looking forward to our trip?'

'It's going to be great. We'll explore Paris and eat at lovely restaurants. We'll see all the sites and treat ourselves to gorgeous things from a boutique.'

'It sounds perfect, mum. We'll find somewhere lovely for your special birthday meal on Monday.'

'Oh yes, of course. I keep forgetting about my birthday.'

'It's a shame Dad can't be here for it.'

'Yes, it is, but your father's not exactly a Paris person, is he?'

'No, I suppose not.'

'We'll have more fun on our own in any case. We always have a laugh when we go away, don't we? Our little holidays are a triumph every time.'

Mary paused to think about the trips they'd been on before. Not one of them had been what one might call a 'triumph.'

'Do you remember when we went to that health farm, hoping for a nice relaxing time, but it turned out to be a military fitness camp?'

'Yes. How could I forget? I thought I'd die from all the exercise.'

'You got your knickers into a right twist, didn't you? Oh, fiddlesticks. Oh damn, and blast. You know what I've done, don't you? I've just realised that I've forgotten my knickers.'

'How do you mean you have forgotten your knickers? And what made you suddenly think of that?'

'It was me saying that you got your knickers in a twist. My mind went to knickers, and I suddenly remembered putting my pants in a little pile on the bedside cabinet, and I could see myself walking out without picking them up. Then Pauline called for a chat so I got distracted. Oh, I am silly.'

'That's okay, you can get some gorgeous new lingerie in Paris,' said Mary. 'That'll give Dad a nice surprise when you get home.'

'I do quite like the idea of buying some lovely knickers in Paris. What a treat.'

'The best lingerie in the world. We must remember to pop into one of those boutiques between visits to the Louvre and the Eiffel Tower. I think it's illegal to come to Paris and not buy something. Is there anything else you want to do while you're here?'

'Not really. How about you?'

'I want a bright red lipstick.'

'Oh, me too. Like the French women wear. A wildly scarlet lipstick that cries out for a Galois in a cigarette holder, long black gloves, a sneering look and a chignon.'

'Wow. You paint quite a picture there, Mum. OK, well, we'll definitely get us both a red lipstick then.'

'And knickers.'

'Of course. Mustn't forget the knickers.'

'Oh, Mary, this is going to be great. What other holidays have we been on together? I can't think now.'

'Mainly camping, and that wasn't so much a holiday as torture.'

'Oy, we had a nice time camping, thank you very much. I remember you enjoying it when you were a little girl.'

'Yeah, not sure. All I remember is that it was always muddy,' said Mary. 'Why did you make me do that? Didn't you like me or something?'

'Don't be ridiculous; we loved you so much. We wanted to spend all the holiday with you, but we didn't have much money back then. Camping was a good way to get out of the house and go on holiday without spending a fortune. We had some fun; you must remember some of the fun we had.'

'I remember going off to Normandy so Dad could see all the beach landing places from the war, like where the D-Day landings took place, then we'd see the Bayeux tapestry.'

'Yes, going anywhere with your father did seem to be connected to the war somehow.'

'What was all that about? Why couldn't we have looked at pretty gardens or visited zoos? Why did we always end up looking at something connected to the war?'

'Oh, it was your father, you know what he's like with the

war. He's fascinated by it. All the men of that generation who were too young to fight in the war but saw their fathers go through it have a natural fascination with the whole thing and feel slightly guilty that they weren't involved.'

'That's interesting,' said Mary. 'I've never thought about it like that before. Do you think Dad felt guilty because his father and uncles fought, but he didn't.'

'Guilty probably isn't the right word, but when you see your father doing something like that, part of you must wish you'd been able to do it. To prove you are a man, I suppose.'

' I guess. Men are peculiar creatures.'

'Human beings are peculiar creatures,' said Rosie as the train shot along.

'No, I think women are perfectly rational and lovely; men are complicated.

For example, Dad couldn't tell his father, 'I'm so proud of what you and your generation did. My generation and I will always be grateful for your sacrifice, strength, and fearlessness.' Could he?

'Well, that's certainly true. Your father would never be able to talk to anyone like that. Your dad is not a very emotional person.'

'No, instead of talking about it rationally, he marched us all off to learn about the battalions of the 919th Grenadier Regiment. Like I said, men are batshit crazy.'

It was remarkable that a comment about knickers on the bedside table had grown into a full-scale debate about the nature of fathers and sons.

'But you know your father loves you very much, right? Whatever happens, he'll always love you.'

'Yes, of course, I know that. Why are you saying that?'

'No reason, said Rosie. 'I'm just saying it because it's true. We both love you very much.'

'And I love you very much.'

The two women smiled at one another and pondered the subject from vastly different viewpoints.

Mary wondered why her mum suddenly said that her father would always love her, 'whatever happens.' What did that mean? Was her dad very ill? She hoped not. The idea of losing him was devastating beyond words. She looked over at her mum, lost in thought.

Rosie was distracted in an entirely different way. Talk of scarlet lipstick and fancy lingerie made her think about how she looked, and the image in the train window to her side did not please her.

Sixty was a difficult age for a woman...she wasn't old by any means, but she wasn't young either, and if she was to face the rest of her life as a single woman, perhaps she needed to pay more attention to how she looked.

As she'd gone through menopause, she had worried more and more about the deepening wrinkles on her face and the way her joints creaked and ached in the morning.

It still alarmed her to walk past a shop window and glimpse the old lady looking back at her.

Inside, she felt no different, but she was suddenly wrapped in a different skin that looked a bit rubbery and was if it needed ironing.'

'What are you thinking about?' asked Mary.

'Oh, nothing. Just the fact that I'm 60 soon, and that's very old.'

'I can't believe you're nearly 60, either. You look about 40. People always think you're my older sister.'

'Well, that's very kind. I try to look nice, but it's much harder when you're older.'

'Then stop trying. It doesn't matter; you're happily married, everything's going swimmingly - no need to worry about all that stuff.

'I can't wait to be old. You can dress like a nutter and

wander around the place in your socks if you like. There's an expectation of eccentricity. If I dressed like a lunatic, the police would come. If you dressed like a mad woman, Vogue would put you on the cover.'

'Ha ha, I'm not sure about that. Don't ever wish to be older, love. It's not all that great.'

'In what way?'

'In every way, like the creaking. Good lord, everything creeks and aches all the time. I'm not in agony or anything, but every little part of me hurts a little bit more than it used to.

'There are so many clicks and clacks from my joints it sounds as if someone's knitting next to me. It's like I'm being serenaded by knitting needles when I used to be serenaded by handsome young men.'

'You are bonkers, mum. I've never heard the knitting needles. You just look like a very attractive woman to me. Ted always says he hopes I look like you when I'm older.'

'That's lovely of him; you've got a good one there, young lady.'

'So stop beating yourself up about your age. It's just a number.'

'Yeah, it's just a number that's as near to 80 as it is to 40. That can't be right, surely. Only five minutes ago, I was 22 with the world at my leopard print, high-heeled feet; now I'm looking in the window at Clarks and thinking how comfortable all the bowling shoes look.'

'Bowling shoes? You never go bowling.'

'No - the shoes that look like bowling shoes. And I don't go bowling because if I turn around suddenly, I have the sort of neck pain that a younger person would associate with severe whiplash from a multi-car pile-up. Honestly, I've injured myself scratching my head more than I've injured myself disco dancing.'

'That's because you don't disco dance.'

'I used to – you should've seen me and your dad when we were younger. We danced like crazy all the time. Back in the days when music was music, not just aggressive young men shouting into the microphone and talking over the background beat.'

'That's called rapping, mum.'

'It may well be…it's certainly not music,' said Rosie.

'Now you're sounding old. I'm going to have to have to put you down if you keep talking like this.'

'It might be for the best.'

CHAPTER 4: CITY OF LIGHTS AND LOVE

'*B*onjour, bonjour,' Mary said to everyone she saw. She hoped they all thought she was charmingly bilingual, but in truth, these were the only French words she knew.

'Slow down, you're going too fast,' said Rosie, struggling to keep up with her runaway daughter.

Mary had a habit of striding purposefully when driving a wheely case. She felt like a lawyer in Suits, ready to strut into the courtroom, save the world, and shout 'objection!' a great deal.

She slowed down when she realised how far ahead she'd gone and waited for her mother to catch up. Once they were side-by-side, they decided the best thing to do was to get a coffee and sample the famous Parisian pastries.

'Here?' said Mary, pulling out a chair at a lovely roadside café and offering it to her mum.

'Oh, how French,' said Rosie, admiring the view

'What are those?' Mary pointed at one of many brightly coloured signs hanging from lampposts and buildings.

Rosie slipped her glasses on and peered out at them.

'Oh, Olympics. It's to do with the Olympic Games,' she said.

'The Olympic Games were held in Paris?'

'Yes.'

'Oh right.'

'You've never really liked sport, have you? Not since you gave up gymnastics.'

'No, not really. I quite like the Olympics, though. I mean, I've no interest in it, but then I find myself becoming an expert in small-bore shooting, and I stay up until 4 a.m. waiting to see whether the Slovakians beat the Tongans or something. I didn't realise it had been in Paris.

'Actually, you know what would make the Olympics much more interesting,' said Mary, stirring her coffee and gazing off into space. 'The Olympics should be open to everyone. You just get a letter in the post telling you what sport you're doing, and you go and do your best.'

'I'm not sure about that.'

'No, bear with me. Just imagine it. Dad gets a letter saying he's in the pole vault competition on Tuesday, so he has to buy himself a big stick and one of those Lycra all-in-one things and turn up to compete. I mean, how much fun would that be?'

'I admit - that would be a lot of fun.'

'It would... Aunty Susan in the judo, Uncle Mark doing synchronised swimming and Pauline from bridge club trying to get onto the beam.'

'I imagine that Pauline would be able to get on the beam, she's incredible.... She does lots of yoga and always looks amazing.'

'Yeah, she does look amazing, she's lovely as well, isn't she? I've always liked her.'

'Me too. Your Olympics idea is nuts though.'

'It's not. I'm sending that idea to the Prime Minister.

There's no reason why they couldn't implement it next time for the next Olympic Games.'

'You do that, love. I imagine the Prime Minister has got nothing else to worry about. Now, finish your coffee and let's get going.'

'OK. Let me just get a picture of this café scene for Insta.'

'For what?'

'I've set up an Instagram account... You know – social media.'

'Oh blimey, I'm not really on top of all that. Pauline does it, though.'

'Come on, Mum. You need to get with it. You just post pictures and things about where you've been and what you've done.'

'And people look at the pictures?'

'That's exactly what they do.'

'Right, well, you can do the Instagrammers, and I'll sightsee. Where do you fancy going?'

'Obviously, we have to visit the Eiffel Tower and the Louvre. Which one first? A giant pylon or a glimpse of the Mona Lisa?'

'I'm not sure I'm in a pylon sort of mood. Shall we go and see Mona?'

ONCE THEY HAD DROPPED their bags at the hotel, they headed straight out.

'I've been to the Louvre before, but it was ages ago,' said Mary. 'I guess I was probably a teenager.'

'Yes. Or even younger than that. I have a feeling you were around 11-years-old.'

Mary knew that she could not fully appreciate the magnificence of the building itself the first time she came.

She stood still as they reached the front, admiring its

WE'LL ALWAYS HAVE PARIS

spectacular beauty. The glass triangular pyramid sparkled in the late morning sun.

'Hands down the second-best triangular pyramid ever,' said Mary.

'Second best? What's the first?'

'Toblerone,' said Mary, without taking her eyes off the building before her. Of course, Toblerone.. What else?'

As they walked through the corridors of The Louvre, Rosie admired the paintings, turning to her guidebook to read more about them while sighing at their beauty and majesty. Mary stood patiently, realising—not for the first time—that she didn't like art.

'Isn't that incredible? Look at the way the colours create movement.'

'Incredible,' said Mary.

'It's such a gift to be able to paint like that, isn't it?' Rosie said.

'Absolutely. Shall we go and find the Mona Lisa?'

'We'll get there, darling. No rush. Wow, look at this one…' Rosie pointed at a dark canvas with morose people doing dull things.

'Look at the way she lifts the water jug.'

'Oh yes,' Mary said, unable to squeeze any joy out of the paintings. Who, on God's sweet earth, cares how a skinny woman in a painting holds a jug, for God's sake?

'Here we are. This is the room, isn't it: Salle des États. This is where the Mona Lisa hangs. It's the biggest room in the gallery. The Wedding Feast at Cana by Veronese is in here, too.'

'Great,' said Mary. She was looking forward to seeing the Mona Lisa, a world-renowned painting. Even Mary recognised that was quite a special thing to do.

'Did you know it's been shown at the Louvre since the French Revolution?'

'I did not know that, mum.'

'Since 2005, it has been kept in a temperature and humidity-controlled glass case.'

'Another thing I had no idea about.'

'Why do you think that is?'

'To protect it?'

'Yes, because it wasn't painted on canvas but on poplar wood, which has warped, and a crack has appeared. They keep it in a special case to make sure it's not damaged further. Do you want to know something else?'

'No. I already know more than I thought any person could know. I could do a degree in fine art. I'm not letting you buy more guidebooks EVER.'

As predicted, a huge crowd had gathered around the painting, and a certain amount of jostling was taking place as people of all ages, nationalities and sizes fought for the best place to stand to see it.

The next issue was that everyone wanted to move to the side while standing before Mona to see whether her eyes followed them. So, even when people found the position they wanted to stand in, a fair number bashed into those next to them, who in turn got very angry.

Mary was reminded of the rare times she'd been to an aerobics class, and when the instructor said 'left', there was always one muppet who went 'right' and bashed into everyone. Worse of all – that muppet was usually Mary.

'It's incredible,' said Rosie, and Mary tried not to sigh. Yes – it was great to see such a famous painting, but to Mary's eyes, it wasn't half as big, impressive or moving as she'd imagined.

'Shall we go and look at some other paintings,' said Mary. 'We can always come back later if we want to see it again.'

'Oh, OK,' said Rosie, dragging herself away from the picture and stopping to consult her guidebook.

'Are you ladies lost?' a strong French accent interrupted them.

'We're just trying to figure out where to go next. There's so much to see,' said Rosie.

Mary watched as the man, wearing a velvet jacket, looked at her mother in such a leery and inappropriate way that she wondered whether she should punch him. Mary was well aware that her mother attracted male attention, which had always concerned her more than it should. For heaven's sake, her mum would be 60 in a few days. Why did so many men fancy her and so few fancy Mary?

No woman should have to stand back and watch as slimy Frenchmen gawped at her mother. Especially not when that woman was in her 30s, at the peak of her beauty. Why were there no Frenchmen breathing Gauloise-scented breath in her direction?

'I take you up the Daru Staircase?' said the man. 'It is quicker that way.'

'You want to take her up the what?' Mary said rather more aggressively than she meant to.

Mrs Brown looked at her daughter sternly. 'He's only being kind.'

'Yeah, right. We'd never see you again if he got you up the Daru.'

'It's OK, thank you,' said Rosie to the man in velvet. 'You are very kind, but we will wander around together. Thank you.'

'But you must have a guide.'

'No,' said Mary. 'We must not have a guide. No guide, thank you.'

The man shrugged and looked so sad about this turn of

events that Mary almost wanted to relent and let him show them around. ALMOST.

'Come on then, Mum.' Mary dragged her mother away from the delights of 16th-century Italian art (or whatever it was. She had long ago lost track of what century and country the art was from. It was all starting to merge into one).

'He seemed quite nice,' said Rosie. 'I don't know why you were so rude to him. Having an attractive Frenchman showing us around would have been nice.'

'You're a married woman, behaviour yourself,' said Mary.

Rosie smiled weakly. 'Come on, let's have a look in here. This is where the really old stuff is.'

Mary glanced at her mother, wondering whether she was joking. Nope. This was where the really old stuff was kept, unlike modern paintings like the Mona Lisa.

'Ah, you have come to look at the sculptures,' said a familiar voice. It was velvet-jacket-man again (let's call him VJM), with his over-styled hair and shiny brogues.

'Let me introduce you to the statue of Ain Ghazal.'

He swung his arm out with a dramatic flourish to show us a rather odd-looking statue that, to Mary's untrained eye, looked as if it had been created by a seven-year-old for a school project.

'This statue is the oldest in The Louvre. It is 9000 years old.'

'9000?'

'Yes. He has aged well, no?'

'Yes,' said Mary, thinking it was astonishing that they would have something 9000 years old. That was insane. 'What was happening 9000 years ago?' she asked.

'There were various civilisations around,' he said. Then Rosie joined in with a fact from her guidebook, and she and VJM spoke over one another, saying exactly the same thing.

'The wheel was invented 7000 years ago.'

'Ha ha. We said the same thing. How funny,' said mum.

'Very funny,' said VJM.

'Not that funny, really,' said Mary.

It seemed to Mary that both of them were laughing way more than the moment warranted.

'We said the same thing!'

'Ha, ha, ha…'

Please give me strength, thought Mary as she noticed her mother going all giddy and smiley in his presence.

'I don't mean to be rude, but we were just having a bit of a mother-and-daughter time here. Do you mind leaving us alone to look round?'

'Of course. I apologise,' he said, stepping back.

'Why are you being so rude to him? I think he's a lovely man, and having someone to show us around would be useful. We don't know where we're going or what to look at; why don't you just let him show us.'

'He's clearly here because he fancies you, and I'm trying to protect you from your baser instincts. Have you seen his jacket? And his shiny shoes? Men who spend that long polishing their shoes are not to be trusted.'

'You are a funny little thing, Mary Brown.'

'There's nothing little about me, mother, but I'm glad you think I'm funny.'

'Come on, there's a door over there. Let's go and investigate and see where it leads.'

CHAPTER 5: THE SPIRAL STAIRCASE

Mary and Rosie pushed against the door. It swung open to reveal a spiral staircase. of steep wrought iron steps. She cast her eyes down to the bottom. 'Will you be able to manage it?' she asked her mum.

'For goodness sake, of course, I will. I'm 59, not 90. I'm in the prime of my life.'

'That wasn't what you were saying earlier, but - OK - come on then. Let's explore.'

So, off they went, grasping the balustrade as they eased their way down in semi-darkness. At the bottom of the staircase was a small wooden door.

'I guess we go through here?'

'Yes, I think so, but I'm not sure we've gone down far enough to reach the next floor; the main staircases are quite long.'

'What do you think this is then?'

'Perhaps it's a storeroom or something? Do you think we should go back up?' said Rosie.

'No, I'm sure we'll find a way through. Let's see what's in here.'

Mary stepped up towards the door and pushed it. There was some sort of clip on the front of it, and when she released it, the door swung open. Inside was a dark, cavernous room.

'Come on, this isn't right. There's no art in here,' said Rosie.

Mary considered a room without art to be a pleasant relief.

She stepped further inside, and all the lights sprang into action.

'I hate movement-sensitive lights; we have them at work. You go to the loo first thing in the morning, and once you've sat down for more than a minute, all the lights go off. You have to sit there, waving your arms like you're air traffic control, to get the light back on,' said Mary.

She turned to look around the room before her and realised it was full of people staring at them.

'I'm so sorry. I'm afraid we got lost. Is it OK to walk through here to get to the next floor?'

The people just sat there looking at her. They all had the same rather blank stare.

'Sorry, we'll go,' said Mary.

'No, please stay. You are very welcome,' said a small, dark-haired woman, walking towards Mary with an outstretched hand. 'Do come in and take a look around.'

'Hi, thank you. I'm Mary. This is my mum, Rosie.'

'Very nice to meet you. My name is Simone.'

It struck Mary that the woman looked like Simone Biles, the brilliant gymnast.

As if on cue, the woman stretched out, lifting her right leg so high into the air that she could touch her ear with it. She was wearing a Team USA leotard.

'Would you like to see my gymnastics?' she asked.

'Sure, ' said Mary, glancing at her mother while Simone

performed a perfect handstand, followed by a backflip and a triple somersault, which sent her soaring into the air. It was like nothing Mary had ever seen before.

'She's good, isn't she?' said another of the people, rising to her feet.

There was something incredibly weird about these people. They *looked* like real people but also looked incredibly unreal.

'This is not right, said Rosie. 'We've landed in some other universe. This doesn't seem right at all. Let's go.'

But one of the many differences between Mary and her mother was that Mary was delighted and enchanted by the unusual while her mother resisted it.

'Let's just stay for a little while,' said Mary. 'Let's see whether there any other athletes here?'

'Me,' said a beautiful-looking man with the softest, most flawless skin Mary had ever seen. He stood up and ran across the room so fast that it was impossible to take in. The speed at which he was going made Usain Bolt look like a pensioner on a walking frame.

'What on earth?' said Rosie. 'That's crazy. How do you run that fast?'

'We can run and jump and swim faster than any human ever,' said the man with perfect skin.

'So, you aren't human?' asked Mary. 'I'm confused. You look human. And you sound human but there's something not quite right.'

'We're humanoid,' said Simone. 'We were created by humans to look like humans, but we are not humans.'

'We are part of a research project,' said a large woman in tight athletics gear. 'I can jump higher than any human; I can jump right into the sky and touch the birds.'

'It's not just athletes. There are scientist humanoids who can understand the universe and everything in it like no person before them. Writers are penning books that are better than any previously written. Humanoids are the future.'

Mary looked at her mother, who looked terrified. 'We really should go,' she said to her daughter. But before either of them could move, a loud creak from behind them caused Rosie to jump.

They both looked around as two security guards walked in and shouted something in French, which neither Rosie nor Mary understood. It sounded aggressive and threatening.

'English,' Mary replied. 'We are English.'

'What you do here? Not good to be here.'

The man sounded more like he came from Eastern Europe than France. He was huge and looked like he had been cast from depleted uranium.

'I'm sorry. We got lost. We just walked in here.'

'How?'

'We pushed the door.'

'Not possible.' The security guards looked at one another and back to Mary.

They were at a stalemate. Mary didn't know what to say. They had, quite simply, walked into the room. The men looked at her as if she had been caught trying to blow up The Louvre.

A familiar man walked in just as the silence and tension began to feel too much. It was Jean Christophe, the guy from the gallery who had been showing them around and showing considerable interest in Rosie.

He spoke to the security guards in French and looked angrily at Rosie and Mary.

'Do you have fingerprint recognition set up?' he asked Mary.

'What? No, of course we don't.'

'Well, how did you get in here?'

'Through the door,' said Rosie.

'This is strictly private and confidential.'

'We didn't know that. Why would it not say 'private' on the door?'

'Because it was securely locked with finger recognition technology.'

'It can't have been - we just walked in.'

'It was.'

This was hopeless. They didn't believe a word she was saying.

'Would you please come with me?' said Jean.

'Where to?'

'To my office so we can discuss this.'

'There's nothing to discuss. You left a door open, and we walked in.'

'Please,' said Jean. 'It would help us enormously if you would come with us to talk it all through.'

'Come on. We might as well go,' said Rosie, grabbing Mary as they left the room, flanked by security.

THEY WERE TAKEN to a grand room and Jean Christophe took a seat behind a massive desk that reeked of self-importance. He smiled at the two women.

Mary watched him closely. He looked much more important, sitting behind his huge oak desk, than he had earlier, chatting to them in the gallery and flirting with Rosie. He'd been charming to the point of irritability back then. Where was all that charm now?

'We would be very grateful if you would sign nondisclosure agreements,' he said.

'OK,' said Mary. 'You understand we have a few questions.'

'Of course,' said AVJM (new name for him - now Arrogant Velvet Jacket Man).

'So—who are you? What are you doing in charge of all this? What did we witness down there? Why was the room so easy to open if it was top secret? Why are you being so rude? Why do you need us to sign anything? Oh - and what's all the heavy-duty security for? Do you think my 60-year-old mother is going to attack you or something?'

'Shhhh about the 60 thing,' muttered Rosie.

Jean Christophe smiled. God, he was slimy.

'I run the future exhibitions for the Louvre. I'm one of the most senior employees here,' he said.

'I thought you were some junior, hassling my mother earlier,' said Mary in an attempt to undermine him a little. He'd become so self-important it was unbearable.

'I was trying to help you understand how important the Louvre is and how special the paintings are. I thought your mother was very charming and knowledgeable.'

'Yes, she's both of those things,' said Mary. 'Can you answer the rest of my questions, like: what do you want us to sign, and why it's so essential.'

'You have just seen some top-secret government projects in development.'

'The humanoids?'

'Yes.'

'You are creating them to beat everyone at sport, and you don't want anyone to know.'

'No, that's not what's going on here.'

'I'm confused. They seemed to be pretty good at sport.'

'Mary, don't get so aggressive. Let's just see what they want us to do, and try and get this resolved,' said Rosie.

'They have been created by the finest minds in French technology: they are powered by AI, and—yes—they are super athletes. But we have other superhumanoids as well.

They are part of a project to understand the human being more fully. They are stored here at The Louvre, but they are the property of the French government.'

'OK. So you haven't created them to win medals at the next Olympics?'

'No, of course not. They represent a vision of what the future could look like. They show the extent to which we can create humanoids who perform like super athletes. We are also creating doctors, technicians, designers, and artists. They show the incredible power of French science.'

'OK. They don't look real though.'

'They will.'

'That sounds dangerous.'

'With the greatest respect, I can't debate this with you any further. I've tried to be open with you, and I have explained what the government is doing. Now I need to get you to sign these,' said Jean, pushing two papers in front of them.

'You know we just walked in there, don't you?' said Mary.

'Yes, we understand that now. We have checked CCTV.'

'So it's all your fault for leaving the door unlocked and unguarded.'

'That was an inexcusable mistake.'

'Would you like to apologise for accusing us of having fingerprint recognition?'

'Of course. I'd like to apologise for any upset caused.'

'So, why can't we leave then?'

'You are free to leave as soon as you sign these forms. They will help us out of this rather sticky situation.'

'So what happens if we sign the forms?'

'Nothing at all.'

'Then, why do we have to sign them?'

'They just stop you from openly discussing what you saw here today, and they protect the security.'

'So, we can't tell anyone?'

'No, you've witnessed a confidential government project.'

'Come on,' said Rosie, leaning over to sign the contract in front of her before her before Mary gently touched her arm.

'Hang on a minute. We need to get these checked out by lawyers first. They are in French. How do we know you're not getting us to sign some ridiculous document?'

'You were the ones that walked into the room. We need to be sure that you will not exploit the situation.'

'Hang on a minute. We walked into that room, looking for a staircase to go down. It's your fault for leaving it open.'

'So are you saying you're unwilling to sign the documents,' he said?

'I'm not saying that. I'm just saying we'd like to get them checked by a lawyer first. I think you should pay all the legal charges.'

Jean Christophe looked weary. 'OK,' he said. 'We can arrange that.'

CHAPTER 7: SIGNATURES & SECRETS

Mary and Rosie were taken to Stibble, Buisson et Feuille solicitors' offices at Place Romeo on Rue de Jus, one of the main streets running into the centre of Paris. The name of the building was a lot more romantic than the building itself. Place Romeo…how beautiful. The building wasn't…just a square block, six stories high and eight stories wide. A big, squat, rather ugly building dumped on the end of an otherwise pretty street. The place was redeemed only by the wrought iron gates at the front, which gave it a more continental feel. But it was disappointingly un-Parisian all the same.

I suppose when it came to matters of the law rather than the stomach or heart, it didn't matter where you were in the world—it was all smart blue suits and big, squat, ugly buildings filled with people on laptops.

They entered the main doors and were greeted by four uniformed men in the entrance hall. French policemen always looked to Mary like fancy-dress policemen…with their revolvers tucked into the belt of their trousers and a baseball cap on their heads. It was what you would wear if you were going to a fancy-dress party as a policeman and didn't have the proper uniform.

The men exchanged greetings and chatted in French. They were talking so fast that she could make neither head nor tail of what they were saying. She didn't hear her or her mother's name mentioned, even though they must have referred to them.

'In here,' said one of the police officers, leading them to a lift, which they all crammed into a very undignified fashion.

About eight of them were in a lift that would have been better suited to four. Still, they couldn't let Mary and Rosie out of their sight, could they? The two women might run through Paris announcing the news about the humanoids.

The whole thing was becoming incredibly bizarre.

'I just want to go out and see Paris now,' said Rosie. 'Maybe we should just sign that NDA and get out of here? I'm sick to death of all this bloody nonsense.'

'Don't worry,' said Mary. We won't be here long. Trust me.'

'Trust you? Trust you?'

MARY AND ROSIE sat uncomfortably in the plush leather chairs of the solicitor's office, feeling out of place among the polished wooden panels and impressive legal tomes lining the walls. The air was thick with tension, and Mary couldn't help but fidget with the hem of her blouse.

'Mum,' Mary whispered, leaning towards her mother, 'I think we should have our own lawyer here. This doesn't feel right.'

Rosie patted her daughter's hand reassuringly, but her eyes betrayed her own uncertainty. 'I know, dear, but let's hear them out first.'

The door swung open, and a tall, impeccably dressed man

strode in, followed by two stern-faced individuals who could only be described as menacing. Mary's stomach clenched as she recognised one of them as the security guard from the Louvre.

'Ladies,' the solicitor began, his voice smooth and practised.

'I understand you've had quite an... unusual experience at the Louvre today. I'm here to help resolve this situation amicably.'

He slid two thick documents across the polished mahogany desk. 'These are standard non-disclosure agreements. If you'll just sign these, we can put this entire misunderstanding behind us.'

Mary's eyes widened as she flipped through the pages. 'But... this is all in French! How are we supposed to know what we're agreeing to? We are here because my mum and I refused to sign any documents we didn't understand, and now you're giving us the same documents again. Unless you are formally detaining us, I'd like to leave, please.'

The solicitor's smile didn't quite reach his eyes. 'I assure you, it's a standard form. Nothing to worry about.'

Rosie cleared her throat, her voice trembling slightly. 'We're not comfortable signing something we can't understand. Perhaps we could have our own legal representation look it over?'

The atmosphere in the room shifted palpably. The security guard from the Louvre stepped forward, his voice gruff. 'Madame, I don't think you understand the gravity of the situation. What you saw today was highly classified. We could be discussing criminal charges if you refuse to cooperate.'

Mary felt a surge of indignation. 'Criminal charges? We didn't break in anywhere! We accidentally opened an unlocked door. How were we supposed to know what was behind it?'

The solicitor held up a placating hand. 'Now, now, let's not get ahead of ourselves. I'm sure we can come to an agreement that satisfies everyone.'

Mary stood up, her chair scraping loudly against the floor. 'No, I'm not signing anything I can't read. This doesn't seem right. We're British citizens, aI'd like to talk to someone at the Embassy.'

Rosie tugged at her daughter's sleeve, trying to calm her down. 'Mary, please, let's not make this worse.'

The room fell silent for a moment. Then, unexpectedly, a new voice joined the fray—a woman standing at the back of the room who hadn't been involved before.

'Perhaps I can be of assistance?'

All heads turned to watch the petite, bespectacled woman adjust her glasses and step into the room with quiet confidence.

'Pardon the interruption. I'm Amélie Dubois, an independent legal consultant. Would you like me to represent you? I believe I can help mediate this situation.'

The solicitor's eyes narrowed. 'Madame Dubois, this is a private matter. Your services are not required.'

Amélie smiled politely but firmly. 'On the contrary, I believe they are. I was asked to attend because these ladies need someone to explain their rights and the contents of the documents you're asking them to sign. Unless, of course, you'd prefer this matter to become more... public?'

The solicitor and the officials exchanged glances, a silent conversation passing between them. Finally, the solicitor nodded curtly.

'Very well. You may review the documents with them.'

Amélie pored over the NDAs for the next hour, translating and explaining each clause to Mary and Rosie. As they delved deeper into the legalities, Mary's initial anger gave way to a mix of fascination and trepidation.

'So, basically,' Mary said, rubbing her temples, 'we're agreeing never to speak about what we saw in that room. The humanoids, the technology, any of it.'

Amélie nodded. 'Essentially, yes. The agreement is quite comprehensive. It even includes clauses about social media posts, personal diaries, and future technological developments that might allow for different forms of communication.'

Rosie leaned back in her chair, looking overwhelmed. 'It seems a bit extreme, doesn't it? All this fuss over an honest mistake.'

The solicitor, who had been silently observing, leaned forward. 'Madame Brown, what you stumbled upon today is of utmost national importance. The technology you saw is set to revolutionise the world. We cannot risk any information leaking before the grand reveal.'

Mary felt a conflicting surge of excitement and unease. On one hand, she was bursting to share this incredible secret, but on the other, she understood the magnitude of what she'd witnessed.

Amélie cleared her throat. 'Ladies, while the circumstances are unusual, I can confirm that the NDAs are legally sound. However, given the situation, we can negotiate better terms.'

Amélie engaged in a heated discussion with the solicitor and officials for the next half hour. Mary watched in awe as the petite lawyer held her ground.

Finally, Amélie turned back to Mary and Rosie with a triumphant smile. 'I've managed to secure some concessions. Instead of signing these extensive NDAs, you'll be allowed to write letters of agreement, including specific legal language they've provided. Additionally, as a gesture of goodwill,

WE'LL ALWAYS HAVE PARIS

they're offering you tickets for a weekend in Paris at Christmas, along with travel and accommodation.'

Mary and Rosie exchanged glances, a mix of relief and excitement washing over them.

'Alright,' Mary said, picking up a pen. 'Let's do this.'

As she began to write, Mary couldn't help but think about the incredible secret she now held. The humanoids, the technology, the grand spectacle of it all. How on earth was she going to keep this to herself?

With a flourish, Mary signed her name at the bottom of the letter, then passed it to her mother to co-sign. As Rosie added her signature, Mary felt a weight lift from her shoulders.

The President of the Louvre, who had been silently observing the proceedings, stepped forward with a smile. 'Mesdames, thank you for your understanding and cooperation. We look forward to welcoming you back to The Louvre very soon.'

As they left the office, Mary linked arms with her mother. 'Well, that was quite an adventure, wasn't it?'

Rosie chuckled, some of the tension finally leaving her face. 'Indeed it was, dear. Though I must say, I'm looking forward to a quiet evening after all this excitement.'

They returned to their hotel, the streets of Paris bustling with life around them. As they walked, Mary couldn't help but notice her mother's subdued demeanour.

'Mum, are you alright? You seem a bit... off.'

Rosie sighed, her shoulders sagging slightly. 'Oh, it's nothing, really. I just... I'm not used to handling these sorts of situations without your father. He's always been my rock, you know?'

Mary squeezed her mother's arm gently. 'I understand. Why don't you give Dad a call? I'm sure he'd love to hear about our adventure... as much as we can tell him, anyway.'

Rosie shook her head. 'No, no. This is our girls' trip. We'll be fine without him.'

Something in her mother's tone made Mary pause. 'Mum, is everything okay with you and Dad? You've been acting a bit strange whenever I mention him.'

'Everything's fine, dear. There's nothing to worry about with your father.'

Mary frowned, unconvinced. 'Then why didn't he come with us? It's your 60th birthday, after all.'

Rosie's eyes darted away, avoiding her daughter's gaze. 'He... he thought we'd have a better time together, just the two of us.'

'But doesn't he want to celebrate with you?'

Rosie's voice grew quieter. 'I think he'd rather that we spent some time together, on our own.'

Mary fell silent, more confused than ever. There was something her mother wasn't telling her, but she decided not to push the issue.

'Shall we get something to eat,' said Rosie. 'I'm starving. We've been in that solicitors' office all day. I need a glass of wine.'

They stopped at a very elegant-looking restaurant and sat outside. While Rosie went to the toilet, Mary's mind raced with the day's events—the accidental discovery, the tense negotiations, and now, this strange undercurrent with her parents. It was a lot to process.

Despite the excitement of their Parisian adventure, there had been a sadness in Rosie's eyes that Mary couldn't quite place. As Rosie returned, Mary figured that whatever was going on between her parents was a mystery for another day. Right now, she needed to make sure her mum had a fun evening.

'I've ordered a bottle of wine,' said Rosie with a smile.

'Blimey, you don't mess around, do you?' said Mary.

'Let's have no more incidents on the trip, shall we,' said Rosie, while Mary nodded.

Little did either of them know, as they sat at the pretty restaurant, perusing the menus, that their Parisian escapade was far from over and that they would have been on adventures beyond anything either of them could have imagined by the end of their trip.

CHAPTER 8: CABARET CAPERS

'Well, that was a fun day,' said Mary as she finished her meal. She'd been eating so much recently, but everything in Paris was impossible to resist… the gorgeous garlic, the crispy frites, the delicious steaks.

'I don't know about it being a 'fun day', but I don't think we should go down any more secret staircases for a while. Did you see those security guards? They were terrifying.'

'No, we won't do that again, don't worry mum.'

'We'll have to make sure we don't tell anyone about the humanoids. You shouldn't even mention it to Ted.'

'Really? I was going to tell the Daily Mail when I got home.'

'No, you can't do that.'

'I'm joking, mum. Relax. We won't mention it again—not to anyone.'

'I can tell Pauline, though, can't I?'

'No, mum. No one at all.'

'But Pauline is very trustworthy.'

'No. We need to forget about it and just pretend it never happened.'

'You know what we should do now, don't you?' said Mary, smiling at Rosie. 'We should go for one more glass of wine before heading home.'

'Oh lovely, yes. I fancy another one. Shall I call the waiter over?'

'No, I've got a better idea. Do you see that there?'

Rosie peered into the streets outside and followed Mary's finger.

'That's the Eiffel Tower, love.'

'No, not that. I know what the Eiffel Tower is. The sign there.'

'La Plume Rouge Cabaret?'

'Yes – come on. It's free before 10 pm, let's go in there and watch some cabaret dancers.'

'Will they have wine?'

'Yes, of course.'

'Will it be obscene? I don't want to see women bouncing ping pong balls out of their bits and pieces or anything nasty like that.'

'Oh my God, mum, of course it won't. Where the hell do you think we are – the back streets of Bangkok? It's cabaret dancing.'

'Just checking.'

'How do you know about ping pong balls.'

'Your father.'

'What?? How does my father know about girls with ping pong balls?'

'He hasn't always been a cardigan-wearing homebody, you know. He used to be quite the man about town.'

'Yeah, sure. He saw it in a documentary, didn't he?'

'I imagine so.'

'Come on, I'll get the bill.'

As they walked towards the cabaret together, linking

arms as they strode down the warm Paris street, Mary couldn't quite believe how things had turned out.

She loved the idea of going to the cabaret. The clubs always seemed so decadent and glamorous from the outside. Rosie was less eager. Indeed, she was still questioning the wisdom of this brave move as they arrived at La Plume Rouge.

'If you don't like it, we'll just leave,' said Mary, pushing through the ornate double doors leading to an intimate foyer. A curved art deco counter dominated the space, behind which stood a smartly dressed maître d' with his hair slicked back so much it looked as if it had been painted onto his head. He sported a thin, precisely trimmed moustache.

To their right, a cloakroom attendant waited patiently, her red-lacquered nails drumming softly on the polished wood of her station. The walls, deep burgundy in colour, were adorned with vintage posters advertising past shows, the faded images of feathered showgirls and dapper gentlemen hinting at the spectacles that lay ahead.

A thick, plush carpet muffled their footsteps as they approached the maître d. He greeted them with a slight bow and inquired about their reservation.

'We 'ave no rezervation,' said Mary, attempting a French accent in the absence of any ability to communicate properly in the language.

'Don't do that; you sound like you're in 'Allo, Allo,' said Rosie.

'Too late. Done it.'

The maître d' flicked his hand into the air, and a man dressed in a dinner jacket arrived promptly. He was as elegant as the maître d', but with his hair pulled back into a man bun rather than glued to his head.

Mary looked at the heavy velvet curtain behind the counter. It rippled slightly, allowing tantalising glimpses of movement and flashes of light from the main room. The muffled sounds of laughter and music teased at what awaited them.

A champagne cork popped somewhere beyond the curtain, followed by a burst of applause. The man smiled at their startled expressions, and with a flourish, he lifted a rope.

'Mesdames, welcome to La Plume Rouge. Please, enter and let the magic begin.'

As they stepped forward, the curtain parted, revealing the glittering world of the cabaret beyond the threshold.

A wave of warmth, music, and laughter enveloped them as they stepped into the cabaret and peered through the darkness in search of a seat. Walls adorned with gilt-framed mirrors reflected the soft glow of crystal chandeliers, their light dancing off sequined gowns and polished champagne flutes.

Rosie's eyes widened, drinking in the spectacle. Her fingers tightened around Mary's arm as she leaned in, her whisper barely audible above the jazz quartet in the corner.

'My God, this is so glamorous. It's like being in the 1940s or something.'

'Well, you should know, mum.'

'Ha, ha. You are so funny. For your information, I was born in the 1960s. Shall we sit over there?'

The place they had chosen was perilously close to the stage, but it was the only completely free table in the room. Mary found her feet moving in time with the rhythm, her body swaying slightly as they weaved between tables. Feather boas brushed against her bare arms as they squeezed past a group of boisterous women.

'This is all so Parisian,' said Rosie, transfixed by a towering drag queen shimmying past in a dress that seemed to be made entirely of sparkling blue sequins.

As they neared their table, the lights dimmed. A hush fell over the crowd, broken only by the occasional clink of ice in a glass. A single spotlight pierced the darkness, illuminating a pair of long, fishnet-clad legs emerging from behind the velvet curtain on stage.

Mary felt Rosie's grip on her arm tighten. She glanced at her mother, catching the reflection of stage lights dancing in Rosie's wide eyes. A smile tugged at Mary's lips as she realised her heart was racing with anticipation.

The master of ceremonies' voice boomed through the speakers, 'Mesdames et messieurs, welcome to La Plume Rouge!'

They sank into their soft, velvet seats and exchanged looks of excited disbelief. The night was just beginning, and already the cabaret had cast its spell. They ordered drinks from a passing waiter and settled back to enjoy the show.

'Mesdames et messieurs, please welcome our stars of the evening – Lady Spandex von Spitzenbuben, Bridget Big Bra von Bourbon, and Flossie Girdle von Cookie!'

Three statuesque figures sashayed onto the stage, each more outrageous than the last. Lady Spandex, true to her name, was poured into a catsuit that left little to the imagination. Bridget Big Bra's ample bosom threatened to escape her corset with each shimmy. And Flossie Girdle? Well, her outfit looked as if it had been made of dental floss—there was barely anything to it—just strings of silk-like material that barely covered the woman's modesty.

As the music swelled, the trio launched into a high-kicking, hip-swinging extravaganza. Rosie clapped along enthusiastically.

'Oh, Mary, isn't this fabulous?' Rosie shouted over the music.

Mary had to admit, it was pretty spectacular. She tipped her drink into her mother's glass, as she had been doing all evening. The dancers flew across the stage, a whirlwind of sequins and sass, their energy infectious. By the finale, Mary and Rosie were on their feet, cheering with the rest of the crowd.

As the applause died down, Rosie grabbed Mary's hand. 'Come on, let's go backstage and meet them!'

'We can't just…' But it was too late. Rosie had drunk too much wine to be argued with. She would meet the cabaret threesome whether Mary approved or not.

They found the dancers in their dressing room, still breathless from their performance. Lady Spandex was the first to notice them.

'What have we here?' she drawled in an accent that was more Bronx than Bordeaux.

'We've come to see you because it's my birthday week, and you were brilliant, brilliant,' said Rosie, staggering as she spoke. 'I'm nearly 60,' she added with a generous hiccup.

'Sorry. I couldn't stop her,' said Mary with a shrug.

'No problem at all. It's wonderful that it's your birthday, but I can't believe you're 60. You don't look a day older than 40,' exclaimed Flossie, her outfit straining as she threw her arms wide. 'We've almost finished for the evening. Just the can-can left to perform. After that, we must celebrate.'

'Oh, the can-can,' said Rosie. 'That's my favourite. I can't wait to see you do that.'

'Have you ever done it?' asked Flossie.

Rosie's face lit up. 'Oh, darling, I haven't kicked that high since… well, never mind when. But I'd love to try!'

Before Mary could interject, Lady Spandex had whisked Rosie behind a shimmering curtain to give her an impromptu lesson.

'You go back to your seat; she'll be with you when we've taught her how to dance.'

That suited Mary, to be honest. She was half the age of

her mother, but she felt tired, and sitting down, listening to music was all she wanted to do. She ordered a glass of orange juice and leaned back against the soft cushions.

Suddenly, the house lights dimmed. A spotlight pierced the darkness, illuminating the heavy velvet curtains. The dancers were back on.

The master of ceremonies' voice boomed through the speakers: 'Ladies and gentlemen, for our grand finale, please welcome our star dancers and a very special guest performer!'

Mary's glass froze halfway to her lips. Surely not...

The first strains of the can-can filled the air. The curtains parted, revealing a line of high-kicking legs. As the dancers spun into view, Mary's jaw dropped. There, at the end of the line, was Rosie.

Her mother's hair had been teased into a wild bouffant adorned with a jaunty feathered headpiece. She wore a corset that seemed to be made entirely of sequins, pushing her ample bosom to new heights. A frilly skirt of eye-watering fuchsia completed the ensemble.

As Rosie high-kicked with enthusiasm, if not precision, Mary noticed her mother's sensible travel shoes had been replaced with precariously high heels. How she stayed upright was a miracle of physics - or perhaps just the power of French wine.

The dancers began their routine, a whirlwind of twirls and high kicks. Rosie, a beat behind and slightly off-kilter, followed along with gusto. Her face was flushed, her eyes sparkling with delight as she attempted to match the professionals' moves.

During a particularly energetic spin, Rosie's headpiece flew into the audience. A bald gentleman in the front row caught it deftly and placed it atop his own head to raucous applause.

WE'LL ALWAYS HAVE PARIS

Mary watched, caught between mortification and hilarity, as her sixty-year-old mother attempted a split. Rosie wobbled and teetered and then, with a look of sheer determination, lowered herself to the floor. The audience held its collective breath.

There was a moment of suspense as Rosie hit the ground, her eyes wide with surprise. Then, triumphantly, she threw her arms in the air, beaming at the crowd. The cabaret erupted in cheers.

The dancers lined up for the final kick line as the music reached its crescendo. Rosie, now back on her feet (thanks to the discreet assistance of Bridget Big Bra), took her place at the end.

'Un, deux, trois!' The count echoed through the room as legs began to rise.

Rosie's leg shot up with unexpected vigour. Unfortunately, her sense of balance didn't quite match her enthusiasm. As her leg reached its zenith, Rosie began to topple backwards.

In a feat of quick thinking, Lady Spandex reached out, catching Rosie's outstretched hand. Instead of falling, Rosie's momentum swung her in a graceful arc, transforming her near-fall into an impromptu cartwheel.

The audience, thinking this was part of the act, went wild. Rosie landed on her feet, wobbling only slightly, a look of utter surprise on her face. Never one to miss an opportunity, she gave a deep, theatrical bow.

As roses rained onto the stage, Mary found herself on her feet, cheering and laughing with the crowd. Her mother might be a sequin-clad disaster, but she was undeniably the show's star.

The dancers took their final bows, Rosie sandwiched between Lady Spandex and Flossie Girdle, her smile threatening to outshine the stage lights. As the curtain fell, Mary saw her mother blowing exuberant kisses to the audience.

She sank back into her chair, equal parts exhausted and exhilarated. One thing was certain: this was a birthday celebration they would never forget.

Mary and Rosie stumbled arm-in-arm back to their hotel as dawn broke over the Paris rooftops.

CHAPTER 9: THE LIPSTICK DILEMMA

THURSDAY:
'Come on, it's getting late; let's go and have some fun,' said Mary, peering out of the hotel at the busy city beyond. They'd had a lie-in that morning after Rosie's exertions the night before, followed by a sumptuous hotel breakfast.

Mary luxuriated in the last piece of thickly buttered toast, observing that you would be hard-pressed to find anything greater than a fried breakfast.

A hotel fried breakfast, in which you could have as much of it as your heart desired, was the stuff of fantasies. Mary knew that if there were such a thing as Heaven, it would be where hotel-style buffets of cooked breakfasts stood on every street corner.

Indeed, the only thing wrong with this morning's was that it wasn't British. The French were adorable; God bless them. But she didn't want pastries and a little pot of jam the size of her thumbnail; she wanted huge amounts of pork-based products and a pile of eggs and beans. English breakfast in the most traditional way possible.

'I fancy a spot of shopping,' she said to her mum, who was enjoying her 95th cup of tea while stretching out her inner thigh.

'I'm not sure,' said Rosie, shaking her head. 'I think it's better if we just stay inside. We can't be trusted in Paris. And I think I might have pulled a groin muscle.'

'I'm not surprised. You're nearly 60 and were doing high kicks and jumping into the splits.'

'Thank God there was no one recording it.'

'Yeah. Thank God,' said Mary, with a smile.

'No, you didn't.'

'Didn't I?'

'You can't have. There were signs everywhere saying that no photography was allowed.'

'I promise not to show anyone,' said Mary.

'I don't believe it. Let's have a look then.'

Mary opened her phone and found one of the many videos she had recorded. 'I didn't get the bit when you first came on because I wasn't expecting to see you in the lineup, but here you are getting ready to start the can-can.'

'GOOD GOD ALIVE,' squealed Rosie.

'You don't look too bad. What are you worried about?'

'Oh, my headdress has gone flying off. Oh goodness. I don't look very steady, do I?'

'Considering the height of those heels, you did very well.'

'Thanks, love. My hair looks great.'

'I know. It suits you.'

'I was silly to run off and join in, though, wasn't I?'

'No, I thought it was fab.'

'But after that ridiculous day we had, with the lawyer and everything. I should have more sense. I should stop drinking so much.'

'No, you shouldn't. You had a great time; that's all that matters.'

'Yes, I suppose so. But let's stay in the hotel today, eat nice food and keep away from anywhere we could cause trouble.'

'Don't be ridiculous, Mum. We didn't cause trouble. You did a lovely dance, that's all.'

'I'm talking about The Louvre.'

'Well, that wasn't our fault. They forgot to lock up the door of their prize possessions. Not our problem that we accidentally wandered in there.'

'Well, it is really. We were trying to escape from the boss at the time. We should've just chatted to him, civilly like I suggested. We might have become friends with him and had free access to the Louvre whenever we wanted.'

'Yes, Mum, that would've been useful, what with us living in Surrey.'

'Who knows, I might have moved out here and had a new life in Paris.'

'What? Living in a threesome with Jean Christophe and Dad? I'm not sure Dad would be in favour of that. Come to think of it, I'm not convinced that Jean Christophe would either.'

'Not everything I do has to involve your father.'

'No, I know, but living with another man might be something he has a view on.'

'Oh, come on. We'll talk about this another time. Let's go shopping.'

'Yay,' said Mary.

Rosie smiled warmly at her daughter. 'But let's not get into any more scrapes. I don't like being in trouble. I'm not the type.'

'I promise mum… No more trouble. Where shall we start? The Champs Elysees?'

'Ooo…very fancy. Will I be able to get some new pants there?'

'Will you stop going on about these bloody pants? We

should be able to get some. They might be lacey and much smaller than you're used to, but there should be lingerie shops on the Champs Elysees. Hey, that sounds great, doesn't it? I might also buy some, just so I can tell people that I bought in lingerie on the Champs Élysées.'

'Yes – it does sound very fancy. Where is it? Do you know?'

Mary pulled out her phone and found the world-famous street. 'Follow me,' she said, and the women strode along towards the wonderful Champs Elysees, which stretched from the Arc De Triomphe to the Place de Concorde.

'GOSH, it's all very French, isn't it?' said Rosie, admiring the lingerie shop in front of them, where delicate pieces of lace and mere whispers of chiffon passed for pants. 'I mean, you wouldn't stay very warm in those, would you?'

'I don't think they're designed with warmth in mind, mother. The people who buy those are thinking of only one thing.'

'Well, when I look at them, I think of only one thing,' said Rosie.

'Oh yes? What are you thinking of then, you filthy mare?'

'Nothing like that. When I look at those, I just think of itching, scratching and discomfort.'

'Yeah, I agree,' said Mary. 'There's nothing sexy about scratching and itching.'

They walked past the shop, noticing that it was predominantly men buying things for women, presumably. The women would then wear the items for the men's pleasure and tolerate the discomfort.

'I like those nice big comfortable cotton pants from Marks & Spencer. You can't beat Marks & Spencer's pants,' said Rosie.

Mary nodded, reluctant to agree with her mother. She wished she was the sort of person who wore ribbons for underwear but entirely agreed with Rosie that a big cotton pant couldn't be beaten.

'Oh look—there's a Tiffany's there,' said Mary, pointing out the beautiful jewellers renowned for their celebrity shoppers and expensive jewels. And Sephora. I love Sephora.'

'What's Sephora? I've never heard of it?'

'It's a big makeup shop with everything you could ever want. I could go in there to get us bright red lipstick. We'll return from this trip with a more Parisian attitude to life. Are you coming?'

'I might just pop in here,' Rosie said, indicating the Zara branch on the other side of the road.

'You can't go in bloody Zara when we're in Paris.'

'Well, I want big pants, and I don't think I'll get those Sephora.'

'I'm not entirely sure you'll get them in Zara either. I'll head over to Sephora, and we catch up here in 20 minutes.'

'Perfect,' said Rosie, kissing her daughter on the cheek and wandering into the Spanish-owned fashion store that can be found on every street in England.

Rosie hesitated at Zara's entrance, her hand lingering on the cool metal handle. The glass doors reflected a woman she barely recognised: silver-streaked hair, laugh lines etched around her eyes, and a slight stoop to her shoulders that wasn't there a decade ago.

She squared those shoulders, took a deep breath, and pushed inside.

A wave of pop music and perfume washed over her. Rosie blinked, momentarily overwhelmed by the kaleidoscope of colours and fabrics surrounding her. Racks of clothing stretched in every direction, a labyrinth of fashion she felt woefully unprepared to navigate.

As she tentatively approached a display of blouses, Rosie saw her reflection in a mirror. Once a prized possession, her cream cashmere sweater now seemed dull and shapeless compared to the vibrant crop tops modelled by mannequins with impossibly long legs. All these windows and mirrors weren't good for the ego.

A group of young English women brushed past, their laughter tinkling like wind chimes. Rosie's fingers tightened on a hanger. She could feel their eyes on her, imagining their whispered comments. 'What's she doing here?' 'Doesn't she know this isn't Marks & Spencer?'

Cheeks burning, Rosie retreated to a quiet corner of the store. She allowed herself to breathe, hidden behind a leather jacket rack. Her gaze fell on a pair of khaki combat trousers. They were beautiful, the kind of thing she would have snapped up in her thirties without a second thought. Now, she hesitated. Would they make her look like she was trying too hard? Like an old woman desperately clinging to youth?

As Rosie debated, she became aware of hushed voices nearby. Two of the young women from earlier were whispering, stealing glances in her direction. Rosie's heart sank. She should leave and find somewhere more 'age-appropriate' to shop. As she turned to go, one of the women approached, a shy smile on her face.

'Excuse me,' the young woman said, her voice warm and friendly. 'I hope you don't mind me asking, but where did you get your cream top? It's gorgeous.'

Rosie blinked, momentarily stunned. 'My... top?' she repeated.

The young woman nodded eagerly. 'Yes! The cut is amazing, and that colour is to die for. My friend and I were just saying how chic you look.'

As if summoned, the friend appeared, eyes sparkling with

admiration. 'We've been trying to work up the courage to ask you all morning. Your whole outfit is just... goals.'

A warmth bloomed in Rosie's chest, spreading outwards until she felt it in her fingertips. She'd been so caught up in her own insecurities that she'd misread their interest entirely. These young women weren't judging her; they were admiring her.

Rosie returned to the khaki combat trousers with a newfound lightness. 'You know,' she said, a mischievous glint in her eye, 'I was just thinking these would look fabulous with my top. What do you think?'

The young women's enthusiastic agreement sealed the deal. As Rosie made her way to the fitting rooms, trousers in hand, she saw herself again in a mirror. This time, she didn't see the grey hair or the laugh lines. She saw a woman with impeccable taste, enviable style, and six decades of life experience that had shaped her into exactly who she was meant to be.

Rosie stepped into the fitting room, ready to embrace this new perspective. Age was just a number, after all, and style? Well, that was timeless.

Ultimately, the trousers didn't fit properly, so she left them and picked up some underwear after taking advice from a shop assistant. The whole experience made her feel much better about herself.

MARY WALKED OVER TO SEPHORA, moving to push the door open before realising it opened itself. She nearly fell through with all the decorum of a hippopotamus. Excellent. Just the sort of look she was aiming for. She walked straight to the lipstick section and pulled out the reddest colours.

She ignored the sales assistant, who looked her up and down. She didn't need any help, and she certainly didn't need any judgement. But as Mary moved to lift out a lipstick called Rouge Incredible, the assistant sprang to life.

'Can help you?' she asked.

'I'm looking for red lipstick, like the ladies of Paris wear.'

'Most ladies in Paris wear nude,' said the woman. 'Just a gentle pink or a nude colour.'

'I want cherry-red lipstick. I want to look like a Parisian from all the films, walking around smoking a Gauloise, wearing a black jacket and black shades.'

'OK,' said the woman.

'Great. So, which lipstick would you buy?'

'I would go for this,' said the assistant, pulling out a nude lipstick. 'It is what we wear in Paris. Everybody wishes to look elegant. Not like a clown.'

'Okay, could you try that on me?' Mary sat on the high stool, expecting the woman to pull out brushes, sponges and cotton buds and make her look tremendous.

But no. She just handed over the rather miserable-looking lipstick and told Mary to try it. The colour was very insipid, a sort of chalky beige. It looked more like a concealer than a lipstick.

'Try,' said the woman.

Mary stroked it across her lips. It felt nice and glossy, and it went on very easily. Perhaps the woman was right. Then she looked in the mirror. My God, she looked ghostly and unwell. It wasn't at all what she was after.

'It is perfect. Now you look Parisian,' said the assistant.

'Do you think so?'

'Oh yes, you look like you come from Paris.'

'But I thought Parisians wore red lipstick. We went to the cabaret last night, and there were many French ladies in beautiful red lipstick.'

'The cabaret? Do you want to look like a chorus girl? No,

ma cherie. You do not want to look like a cheap can-can dancer. This lipstick is much better.'

'Okay, I'll buy it,' said Mary, against her better judgement.

The lipstick was wrapped up, and Mary strode out of the shop with her new purchase. She glanced in the mirror as she went. The lipstick was so pale it made her look more like a cadaver than a French siren.

As she left the shop, Mary opened the door for two French women. Both of them were wearing the exact cherry-red lipstick that Mary had so desired. They looked amazing. That was how she wanted to look, for Christ's sake.

Perhaps should take it back a bit later, at the end of the shopping trip, when another assistant was around.

For now, though, she needed to try and find her mother, which wouldn't be easy. The quiet street she'd left when she entered the store was suddenly chaotic.

Where had all these people come from? There were tons of them, chanting, shouting, and waving banners. What the hell had happened in the 10 minutes it had taken her to buy a bad lipstick?

CHAPTER 10: ACCIDENTAL ACTIVISTS

Mary could see her mother over the other side of the road, clutching a small Zara bag and looking up and down, as confused about the sudden arrival of thousands of campaigners as Mary was.

Mary rang her mum's mobile, fairly sure that her mother wouldn't pick up the call. This is the thing with mothers, isn't it? They may carry phones, but are they ever available when you call them? Do they ever reply to texts? Why do they have phones in the first place?

Mary waved at her mother but couldn't catch her eye, so she edged towards the front of the people gathered, shouting chants on the side of the road. She couldn't understand what they were shouting about or what any of the flags represented.

Football, perhaps?

Perhaps they were campaigning to ensure that shop assistants always gave decent lipstick advice. She'd join that march.

'Mum,' she tried again, bellowing at the top of her voice. It was no good.

She texted Rosie to tell her she was on the other side of the road and would attempt to cross. As she pushed forward to try and cross, she saw her mother dig into her bag, hopefully reaching for her phone.

But then things went horribly wrong. By pushing herself forward, Mary had thrust herself into the throng of campaigners and found herself being dragged down the road with the chanting mob. Police shouted at them as they walked along, but Mary had no idea what on earth they were shouting or what march she was in. She pulled out her phone again and sent another text.

'Mum, it's chaos outside the shop; I'm being pushed down the road in the middle of the demonstrators toward the Arc de Triomphe. Can you head for there?'

Mary attempted to look back over her shoulder, but there was no sign of her mother.

At least there was a plan…she'd get to the Arc de Triomphe and look for her mother there. Now, she just needed to work out what they were marching about. She looked closely at the people around her. Some wore fluffy ears or gloves like paws. She noticed one with her face painted like a woodland creature. What the hell demonstration was she involved in?

She looked further afield. Several of the campaigners were dressed like badgers. Was this a badger march of some kind? Perhaps they were marching to save the badgers from a cull?

That was OK. It was certainly better than being in a march that she didn't agree with or one that could potentially see her thrown behind bars. Surely no harm could come to a woman in pale lipstick inadvertently drawn into a badger march?

While Mary walked along quite happily, surrounded by

people in various stages of badger-dom, Rosie felt slightly more stressed by her situation.

She had retreated from the crowds, and backed into the entrance of Zara, where she read the text from Mary.

She would go to the Arc de Triomphe and meet Mary there. She looked into the throng of people pushing their way down the street, many dressed as furry animals. Everyone was packed in next to one another.

She didn't fancy it at all.

So, instead of following the march down the Champs Elysees, she cut through, past the station they had arrived at a short time ago, and took a different route to the Arc de Triomphe, up a parallel road.

She would get there more quickly and could look out for Mary once she arrived.

Rosie strolled around the corner, away from the throng, swinging her bag from Zara. (She wasn't sure about the knickers she'd bought. The shop assistant had insisted that all Parisians wore knickers like that, but they seemed oddly shaped and made of peculiar material. She might go back there later, when a different shop assistant was working, and change them.)

As Rosie arrived on the parallel road, she noticed a crowd gathering ahead of her. Presumably, more stuffed animals were marching through the streets.

What in the name of the Lord could they possibly be protesting about?

She attempted to push through the protesters, but no one was willing to move to let her through. They seemed like an aggressive bunch, with none of the jollity she'd witnessed on the Champs Elysees.

Certainly, none of them seemed to be dressed like stuffed animals. The rage in their voices and the anger as they punched the air and chanted slogans took Rosie aback. Was this the militant division of the 'Save the Bunnies' campaign?

Rosie also noticed that there were mainly young men in this group, and the tension building up between them and the police who were trying to surround them was palpable. When she'd seen them go up the Champs Elysees, there had been lots of young women, and they had been laughing, chatting, and joking. Who were these guys?

She edged her way to the front of the procession as it approached the Arc de Triomphe.

Police horses drew up on either side of Rosie's gang, and people around her began screaming at them and hitting the officers with their flags and banners. The air of tension grew, but there was nowhere for Rosie to go. She was trapped—surrounded by screaming hooligans on one side and police horses on the other side. She tried to step to the left but was bellowed at by a large man with a shaved head. This wasn't quite the Parisian experience she was hoping for.

ON THE OTHER side of the police horses, Mary was having a lovely time. A woman called Francois was telling her all about the plight of badgers. She spoke in broken English, and adorable animal noises punctuated the story.

The women had sweets on them, which they happily handed out. This was all rather jolly. If only her mum could find a way through to join them, everything would be fine.

But then, a change of mood swept through the crowd, and the furry animals stopped jumping and shaking their tales. No whiskers were pawed, and no sweets were offered.

Chatter started in the group. 'This is not good,' said Francois. 'There is another march today, and it is from the French nazi party. They are always so violent. Always trouble. The police are working hard to keep us all apart.'

Mary had visions of being 'kettled' with a bunch of right-wing troublemakers. She wished she could see her mum to check she was OK. She looked down at her phone; still no response from her. She looked over at the right-wing demonstrations and the line of police horses trying to keep them in check. Riot police were arriving in droves.

That's when she saw Rosie. She'd expected her mum to be further back in the animal welfare march, but, instead, she was right at the front of the Nazi march.

Rosie clutched her Zara bag as if her life depended on it, surrounded by right-wing sympathisers waving swastikas.

'Oh my God, that's my mum,' screamed Mary. 'There. Between the swastika and the bloke with a tattooed face.

'Noooo...' said Francine. 'This is the mother of you?'

'Yes - mother of me.'

'You mother is Nazi.'

'Yes,' shouted Mary.

'She is Nazi? This is terrible.'

'No, no, no. She's not a Nazi. She's with the Nazis.'

'Why she is with them?'

'She's looking for me. She must have walked into the wrong march and got stuck there.'

'This is not good. These is bad people.'

'I know.'

'Mum, Muuuuuum,' called Mary, desperate for her mother to hear her.

The others joined in, shouting in their lovely lilting accents: 'Mother of Mary. Come to us...'

'Mother. Come here.'

But Rosie neither heard the shouts nor saw her daughter standing on tiptoes and waving at her. Even if Rosie had seen her daughter and her new Parisian friends dressed as badgers, there was no way she could have reached them. The police had, by now, arrived in numbers and seemed to concentrate the majority of their resources on Rosie's side of the street.

'When can we go?' asked Rosie, shouting up to the policeman, high on his horse - physically and symbolically.

If he understood her, he decided not to answer. By the look on his face, he didn't know what she was talking about. He gave a Gallic shrug and pushed her back into the throng.

But Mrs Brown was having none of it. She felt annoyed at how everything was playing out on the trip so far – she was worried about the scene at The Louvre and concerned that she'd embarrassed her daughter by can-canning until dawn. She was angry that her marriage was folding before her, that she couldn't bring herself to tell Mary, and that she now seemed to be the lone woman in a sea of young men on a right-wing march through Paris. She'd had dreams of coffee and croissants on the Champs Elysees, not a punch-up with a guy sporting a swastika on his face.

'Can I go through to my daughter?' Rosie tried, pointing ahead to the march she knew her daughter must be caught up in.

'I need to go through.'

The policeman shrugged again, so Rosie pushed forward, nudging the horse's head out of the way and throwing herself towards the badger march opposite.

All the officers present immediately translated this as an act of aggression. 'Arête!' screamed the policemen.

Rosie realised that they were shouting at her to stop, but she had no plans to do so - she continued to drive through, like a prop forward with the try line in sight. She was a magnificent sight, barging through the skin-headed youths, waving her Zara knickers before her as a shield, a middle-aged heroine in beige Marks and Spencer separates.

'I will not be stopped,' she cried as they stopped her.

She was lifted off the ground by two officers while her feet still whirred, cartoon-like below her.

'Let me go,' she raged.

While Rosie struggled, Mary scanned the horizon, looking for her mother. Where had she gone now? She was there a minute ago. As she looked, she locked eyes with one of the men - he stared at her, and she stared back, slowly raising a middle finger. He raised his fist, and she raised hers, snarling at the man. She felt confident in her safety because of the police presence around them, but the way he was staring now was quite scary...she turned away from him abruptly

Then, she saw her mother's familiar form. She watched in awe and wonder. Her mother was struggling and shouting as officers led her out of the march, presumably to safety.

'She's there,' shouted Mary.

'My knickers!' shouted Rosie. 'I dropped them.'

CHAPTER 11: THE CALL HOME

Mary slumped on the bed – tired, dishevelled and in desperate need of a chat to her husband.

'How was your day, then?' asked Ted. 'Have you been doing lots of sightseeing and dining out in ludicrously glamorous places while I've been working for a living?'

Oh, how naive he was to think that a mother and daughter would head to Paris for a gentle, sublime time.

'Unfortunately, it hasn't been quite like that,' said Mary. 'I mean – that's what we were hoping to do, but we got caught up in a big march through the streets of Paris today.'

'What do you mean 'got caught up in'.'

'Exactly that. Mum and I wanted to go into shops on the opposite side of the street, so Mum went off to her shop, and I went to mine; when we came out, there was a big march going past, demonstrating against a badger cull. I accidentally joined in, and Mum accidentally joined a right-wing, Nazi-style march and was almost arrested for head-butting a police horse.'

'Wo Wo Wo. What do you mean - head-butting a police horse? She head-butted a police horse? Your mum?'

'No, mum insists that she didn't do any such thing, but she pushed past the police horse when there was a policeman on him, and the police officer said she head-butted the horse.'

'Blimey, your mum must have a dark side to her that I've never seen before. I can't imagine Rosie head-butting anyone, let alone a horse. That's quite amusing, actually.'

'Hopefully, you'll find it just as amusing when she gets a criminal record.'

'A criminal record, what are you talking about?'

'The police took her details. I thought they were going to take her into custody, but the march was turning into a bit of a riot, so they let her go, but they told her that someone would contact her.'

'Blimey. OK, well - I wasn't expecting any of that. How are you?'

'I'm fine. I had a nice time with a whole load of women dressed as badgers. We were having a fun time, actually... until the Nazis arrived.'

'Yeah, well. I imagine that would put a dampener on things.'

'And I bought a lipstick that isn't anything like the lipstick I wanted.'

'Oh, OK. Well - probably not the best day then. Did you have a good time last night? I tried calling you but couldn't get an answer.'

'Yes – last night was brilliant fun. Mu got drunk and did the can-can at a cabaret club.'

'Ha, ha. Yes, very good.'

'I'm telling you the truth. Hang on, I'll send you the video now.'

Mary opened her phone and sent the small film of her

mother on stage that she had faithfully promised never to send to anyone.

'Has it arrived?'

'Yes, just now. Hang on…let's have a look at this.'

The phone went quiet for a moment.

'Good heavens above. That's your mum.'

'I know.'

'On stage.'

'Yep.'

'In a headpiece and high heels.'

'Indeed.'

'Wooooah…the headpiece has just gone flying off.'

'Yes.'

'That's brilliant. Wow. I'm impressed. Tell me nothing else like that has happened. You've only been gone a couple of days.'

'Yeah, no. Not really. We managed to get into a bit of trouble in the Louvre, but nothing much, honestly.'

ROSIE PACED AROUND her small room with all its shabby-chic furniture and gilt finishings. It was so Parisian. Tonight, she and Mary were going out to dinner, and she was determined to talk to her daughter about the marriage breakup.

Mary kept asking whether anything was wrong; it was up to Rosie to explain properly.

She looked into the mirror at her rather pale complexion and the many signs of age that had crept into her skin as the years had passed. She did what she always did and held up her eyebrows with her fingertips, pulling down the skin underneath her eyes with her thumbs and pulling it towards her ears. She looked back into the mirror… All the lines were gone.

To be fair, she looked like some ridiculous woodland

creature – a marmoset or something - with unfeasibly large eyes and pulled-back lips. But the more she looked, the more she liked her new reflection. She'd rather look like a marmoset than an old woman.

Her phone rang on the small white dressing table in front of her, so she let go of her skin, watching her face wobble back in on itself like ripples of jelly. She looked older and more jowly than ever.

On her phone's screen, she saw her husband's name. He was undoubtedly ringing to discover how Mary was taking the news of the imminent separation. She would have to explain to him that they hadn't spoken about it yet. He wouldn't like that one bit. He was very keen for Mary to know what was happening before the news leaked and she heard it from someone else.

'Hello,' she said.

'How are you doing?' her husband replied in his familiar voice. The sound of him moved something deep within her. She felt like she might burst into tears. They'd been together for as long as she could remember. it seemed hideous that they were splitting up.

'Yes, all fine here. We're having a lovely time.'

'How did Mary take the news?' he asked.

He didn't want to talk about the trip to Paris or ask how her birthday celebrations were going—he was only interested in whether she had spoken to their daughter.

'I haven't told her yet,' said Rosie, pulling back the skin on her face once more as she looked into the mirror.

'You haven't told her? Why not?'

'It's not been the most straightforward of days. There were these protests, and we got caught up in them. I was stuck next to all these lunatics, and I was accused of punching a horse in the head, and then I lost my knickers.'

'You what? You lost your knickers? What the hell, Rosie?'

'No - I wasn't wearing them. I'd bought them and had them in my hand, and somehow, they got lost. But that's not the important bit. It just all went a bit wrong.'

'And what was that other thing you said? You head-butted a horse? Why would anyone head-butt a horse?'

'The guys all had tattoos on their faces, and I wanted to get away. I didn't head butt, I just pushed past the horse.'

'This is insane. I'm coming out,' said Derek, firmly.

'There's no need for that. I'll talk to Mary tonight.'

'No, you won't. You know you won't. I'll be on the train tomorrow morning. I'll send you the details once I know which one.'

Rosie remained silent.

'Are you there, Rosie?'

'Yes, I'm here.'

'I'll see you in the morning.'

'Sure.'

CHAPTER 12: MADAME FIFI'S LINGERIE EMPORIUM

FRIDAY:
The morning sun cast a golden glow over the cobblestone streets of Paris as Mary and Rosie settled into their seats at a quaint café on the Left Bank. The aroma of freshly baked croissants and rich, dark coffee wafted through the air, mingling with the faint scent of cigarette smoke from a nearby table.

Mary cupped her hands around her steaming café au lait, inhaling deeply. 'I feel like a romantic poet,' she said, her eyes sparkling with excitement. The wrought-iron chair creaked slightly as she leaned back, taking in the bustling scene around them.

'Mmmmm... It is lovely here.' Rosie lifted her face to the sun, closing her eyes as she savoured the warmth on her skin. A gentle breeze rustled the leaves of the plane trees lining the street, carrying with it the distant sound of accordion music.

This was how Paris was supposed to be. She felt like she was in a film.

Mary's gaze wandered to a group of art students sketching at a nearby table, their pencils scratching softly against thick paper. 'Did you know that the Left Bank is where all the writers and artists used to gather? I think just by being here, I will absorb some of that creativity and become a modern-day Shakespeare.'

'You might do. Did I tell you that Pauline is going to write a novel? She's got it all planned out.'

A waiter in a crisp white apron glided past, balancing a tray of delicate pastries. Rosie watched him go before turning back to her daughter with an amused smile. 'I'm not sure she'll get around it. I imagine it's quite hard to write a book,' she said, her voice tinged with affection for her friend. 'Anyway, before you start writing sonnets – I have some news for you.'

Mary's eyes lit up, her curiosity piqued. 'Ooohh... news. How exciting.' She leaned forward, nearly knocking over the small vase of fresh daisies on their table.

'Well, I hope you'll think it's exciting; your father's joining us.'

Mary's eyebrows shot up in surprise. 'He's coming to Paris? Are you sure?'

'Yes - he said he was last night.'

'And he's coming out here on his own?' Mary's voice was a mix of disbelief and amusement. 'I've never heard anything like it before. I didn't know that Dad could find the kitchen without assistance, let alone Paris.'

A group of pigeons strutted past their table, pecking at crumbs on the pavement. Rosie shooed them away with a gentle wave of her hand. 'He's arriving this afternoon.'

Mary grinned, her eyes dancing with mischief. 'OK, well, I hope he's willing to head-butt horses and join the can-can, or he will feel very left out.'

Rosie's cheeks flushed at the memory. 'It wasn't a head-butt.'

'I know, I know. I'm just teasing you.'

A street performer's violin sang out from the corner, its melancholy tune weaving through their conversation. Rosie's expression grew serious. 'Look, I'd like you to go and meet your father this afternoon. I've WhatsApped a copy of his ticket so you know where and when he gets in. Is that OK?'

'Yes, of course.'

Rosie hesitated, then reached into her bag. 'And could you hand him this note when you see him?'

She pushed the envelope across the table so cautiously that Mary felt like she was involved in some sort of drug deal. The crisp white paper stood out starkly against the table's weathered wood.

'Of course.' Mary's brow furrowed with concern. 'Mum, is everything OK?'

'Yes, love.' Rosie's smile didn't quite reach her eyes. 'Shall we head off now?'

They paid for their coffee and set off down the narrow street, their footsteps echoing off the centuries-old buildings. The air was filled with the melodic chatter of Parisians going about their day, punctuated by the occasional honk of a car horn or the clatter of a delivery truck.

As they walked back to the hotel, they fell into a companionable silence, admiring the sunlight dancing across the rippling surface of the Seine. Stone bridges arched gracefully over the water, their weathered facades reflected in the river below. A tour boat glided by, the guide's voice drifting up to them as he pointed out the sights to a group of eager tourists.

Along the cobblestone quays, an elderly man in a smart jacket unfolded his newspaper, doffing his cap as they passed. It felt as if all humanity was out to play; joggers weaved through the crowds, and dogs tugged at leashes, eager to explore every scent along the river's edge. A young couple strolled hand in hand, pausing to share a kiss beneath the shade of a chestnut tree.

'I think we can cut through here,' said Rosie, guiding Mary down a narrow side road. The street was lined with charming old buildings, their facades a mix of pale stone and pastel-painted plaster. Window boxes overflowed, adding splashes of colour to the weathered walls.

Along the way were a couple of small boutiques, one of which was a rather dated underwear shop. Its faded awning proclaimed **Madame Fifi's** in elegant script, and the window display featured mannequins wearing undergarments that seemed frozen in time.

'Knickers!' shouted Rosie as they passed it, her voice echoing off the buildings.

'It's worth a try,' said Mary, eyeing the dusty window sceptically. The place looked so ancient that it seemed unlikely they'd have anything Rosie wanted to wear.

The bell above the door tinkled as Rosie and Mary entered Madame Fifi's. The scent of lavender and mothballs hung in the air, mingling with the musty smell of old fabric. Faded posters of 1950s pin-up girls adorned the walls, their coy smiles at odds with the outdated undergarments on display.

A silver-haired woman in a high-necked blouse emerged from behind a velvet curtain, her heels clicking on the worn wooden floor. 'How may I assist you, mesdames?' Her voice was thick with a French accent.

Rosie cleared her throat, her cheeks turning a delicate shade of pink. 'I need some new knickers, please.'

'Mais oui! Follow me.' The assistant led them to a rickety display case, its glass clouded with age. She withdrew a flesh-coloured monstrosity, holding it aloft like a prized trophy. 'Our finest girdle, guaranteed to – how you say - smoothing lumps and bumps.'

Rosie's eyes widened in horror. Mary stifled a giggle, her shoulders shaking with the effort.

'Er, perhaps something... less restrictive?' Rosie suggested, her voice strained.

'Of course!' The woman disappeared behind the curtain once more, the rustle of fabric accompanying her search. She returned triumphantly with what appeared to be a parachute adorned with lace. 'Very practical,' was her only comment as she held it up for inspection.

Mary's shoulders shook with silent laughter. Rosie elbowed her, trying to maintain her composure.

'Maybe something... smaller?' Rosie squeaked, her face now a brilliant shade of red.

The assistant's face lit up like the Eiffel Tower at night. 'Ah! I have just the thing.' She scurried off, disappearing once more behind the threadbare curtain.

Rosie turned to Mary, her voice a desperate whisper. 'If she brings back a chastity belt, we're leaving.'

Mary wiped tears from her eyes, gasping for breath. 'I can't breathe!'

The curtain swished open with a flourish. 'Voilà!' The assistant triumphantly held up a pair of knickers festooned with an explosion of ruffles and bows. The garment looked like it belonged in a Moulin Rouge costume closet rather than a practical underwear drawer.

Rosie's jaw dropped, her expression a mix of horror and disbelief. 'I'm not doing the can-can at the cabaret again. I just want some nice, comfortable M&S knickers.'

'You like?' asked the assistant, her smile unwavering as she dangled the frilly creation before them.

'They're not for us, but thank you,' said Mary, stifling another laugh as she gently led her mother to the safety of the street.

The sounds of Paris enveloped them once more as they stepped out of the shop, both struggling not to laugh. The aroma of fresh baguettes wafted from a nearby boulangerie, making their mouths water despite their recent embarrassment.

'I bet you regret forgetting your knickers now, don't you?' said Mary as they entered the hotel's reception. The lobby blended old-world charm and modern luxury, with gleaming marble floors and a grand chandelier overhead.

Rosie sighed, shaking her head. 'You can have a look for me this afternoon when you go to pick your dad up from the station. They have some proper shops there with clothing for people of my age.'

Mary saluted playfully and headed towards the elevators. The soft ding announced its arrival, and she stepped inside.

'Oh, and love - don't be late!' Rosie called after her. 'You know how your father hates going abroad. I don't think he's ever been abroad on his own before. Be there to meet him, or he won't be able to cope.'

'Don't worry. I will!' Mary's voice echoed back as the elevator doors began to close.

'And - the note.' Rosie's reminder slipped through just before the doors shut completely.

'Yes, I'll give him the note,' came Mary's muffled reply.

Rosie walked up to her room, choosing to take the stairs rather than the lift, smiling to herself all the way. She'd given Mary a note to hand to Derek, asking him to buy the knickers she wanted. She'd done this not just because she wanted the knickers but also because this would be the worst assignment she could set him. He would loathe going into a women's clothes shop, particularly loathe stepping into the lingerie section, and have heart palpitations about looking at ladies' underwear.

The small things made you smile when your whole world was crumbling beneath you, she thought as she closed the door behind her. The room felt suddenly empty and quiet, starkly contrasting the vibrant city outside. Rosie sat on the edge of the bed, the weight of unspoken worries settling on her shoulders like a heavy cloak.

For a moment, she allowed herself to feel the full force of her concerns – about Derek, their marriage, and the future that suddenly seemed so uncertain. But then, with a deep breath, she straightened her shoulders and stood up. There was Paris to explore, after all, and a daughter to cherish. Whatever storms lay ahead, she would face them with the grace and strength that had carried her this far.

Rosie opened the curtains with renewed determination, letting the Paris sunshine flood the room. The City of Light sparkled before her, full of promise and adventure. She had chosen this trip for a reason and intended to make the most of every moment – bittersweet though some might be.

CHAPTER 13: DEREK'S MORTIFYING MISSION

The bustling streets of Paris hummed with life as Mary navigated her way through the maze-like alleys of Montmartre. Rosie's WhatsApp message echoed in her mind, its instructions clear as day:

'You walk to the end of the road, to the small cafe where we had coffee. From there, you can't miss The Metro. You get on it and get off at Gare de l'Est, which is five minutes from Gare du Nord. Then you look to see what platform the train from St Pancras comes in, and you hover on the concourse near that platform until your father arrives.'

It couldn't be clearer. Or so Mary had thought.

Yet here she was, surrounded by a sea of white-painted faces and black-and-white striped shirts. The cobblestone square buzzed with the silent energy of mime artists, their exaggerated gestures painting invisible stories in the air. The scent of acrylic paint and sweat hovered around them.

Mary's heart raced, a mix of anxiety and embarrassment coursing through her veins. How had she ended up here, so far from her intended destination?

'Where are we? I'm looking for the metro; I think I'm lost,' she said to one of the white-painted, odd-looking mime artists. The words tumbled out in a rush, her British accent standing out starkly against the backdrop of French chatter.

The mime artist gave her a surly sideways glance, his painted eyebrows arching in what could have been amusement or annoyance. Mary felt her cheeks flush.

'Oh yes – sorry, I forgot you're not allowed to speak.'

She laughed nervously as the man raised his hand slowly, pointing an overly long, skeletal finger towards a point in the distance. The gesture was so dramatic it seemed almost comical, yet Mary felt a surge of relief.

She followed his finger's direction, squinting against the bright Parisian sun. 'Where was he pointing? Ah. The main road. And a Metro stop. Perfect.'

'Thank you so much,' she said, turning back to the man. His painted face remained impassive, but his hand moved, gesturing towards a battered top hat at his feet. Coins glinted inside, catching the sunlight.

'Why, of course,' said Mary, fumbling in her purse and dropping a note into his hat. The crisp paper fluttered down, landing softly atop the coins. 'How on earth do you stand like that for so long? You must get so fed up. I'm a real fidget. I couldn't do it.'

The silence stretched for a moment, broken only by the distant sound of an accordion and the chatter of pigeons. Then, to Mary's utter shock, the mime's stoic facade cracked.

'God's sake, love, can't you see I'm trying to be a statue here?' The words burst forth in an unmistakably English accent, tinged with exasperation.

Mary's jaw dropped. 'Oh my God, you're from England. I assumed you were all French.'

'No, a few of us are English,' the man replied, his voice low as if trying not to break character completely.

'Where are you from?' Mary asked, curiosity overriding her initial shock.

'A place called Esher, in Surrey. You wouldn't know it. Very suburban.'

Mary's eyes widened. 'I know it very well. My God, my husband and I live in Hampton Court. I work at the big DIY and gardening centre in Cobham.'

The mime's painted eyebrows shot up, genuine surprise breaking through his makeup. 'No way! That's so weird. My brother is the manager there.'

'Who? Keith?'

'Yes – do you know him?'

'My God, yes. That's so incredibly strange. He's my boss.'

The conversation unfolded like a surreal dream, the backdrop of Paris fading away as this bizarre connection to home emerged. Mary found herself caught between laughter and disbelief.

'I hope he's a good boss,' the mime said, a hint of brotherly pride in his voice.

'Yes – he's great. We all love him,' Mary lied smoothly, her customer service skills kicking in automatically. In reality, Keith was a knob. No one liked him. But here, in this strange moment in Paris, it seemed kinder to maintain the illusion.

'Glad to hear it. I'd love to chat, but I need to get still, or I won't earn any money today.' The mime's voice took on a note of regret, the real world intruding on their surreal encounter.

'Of course, completely understand,' she said. 'Nice to meet you.'

As the mime resumed his statue-like pose, Mary found herself oddly compelled to try it too. She stood beside him, attempting to mimic his stillness. The sounds of Paris washed over her – the melodic French conversations, the distant rumble of traffic, the cooing of pigeons. She focused on her breathing, trying to channel the mime's zen-like calm.

A young family approached, their little boy's eyes wide with wonder at the 'statues'. The child, no more than five or six, reached out a tentative hand and prodded the mime's leg. Mary watched in awe as the man remained perfectly still, not even a flicker of movement betraying him.

Emboldened by his success with the first 'statue', the boy turned to Mary. His small finger jabbed at her leg, and Mary's carefully cultivated stillness shattered.

'Ouch!' she squealed, the sound piercing the tranquil square. The boy squealed too, jumping back into his mother's arms and bursting into tears. The family's laughter mingled with the child's sobs, creating a cacophony that drew stares from passersby.

'I'm not a real statue,' Mary explained hastily, her face burning with embarrassment. 'I'm just trying to keep still.'

The father, still chuckling, said something in rapid-fire French and tossed a banknote at her feet. Mary bent to retrieve it, the crisp paper cool against her fingers. With a flourish, she dropped it into the real mime's hat, blowing him a kiss before hurrying away in search of the elusive Metro station.

The streets of Paris seemed to shift and change as Mary made her way towards Gare du Nord, the earlier detour having thrown off her sense of direction. But finally, the imposing facade of the station loomed before her; its grand clock face a silent reproach for her tardiness.

As she entered the cavernous space, the sounds of the city gave way to the echoing announcements and the rhythmic clack of luggage wheels on tiles. The air was thick with the mingled scents of coffee, pastries, and that indefinable essence of travel.

Mary's eyes scanned the crowd, searching for the familiar

figure of her father. She spotted him almost immediately, his back to her as he sat in a café. A pang of guilt shot through her as she realised how long he must have been waiting.

She approached quietly, the image of her father's usual self - all cardigan-clad and armchair-bound – at odds with the man she saw before her. This version of Derek Brown seemed... different. More at ease, somehow.

Mary laid her hands on his shoulders, leaning in close. 'Boo,' she shouted, her voice cutting through the station's ambient noise.

Derek turned, his face breaking into a warm smile. 'Ah, there you are. Ooh... your lips are a funny colour. Are you OK?' he asked, his tone casual, as if popping over to Paris was something he did most days.

Mary blinked, taken aback by his nonchalance. 'Yes, my lips are fine – just made an odd makeup choice.'

Then, she spotted the Gauloises cigarette languishing in the ashtray before him, a thin trail of smoke curling upwards. The acrid scent hit her nostrils. This was all so at odds with her father's usual behaviour.

'I didn't know you smoked,' she said, her voice tinged with surprise.

Derek shrugged, a mischievous glint in his eye. 'When in France, my love,' he said, gesturing for her to sit. 'Give me a kiss.'

Mary hesitated, caught between the urge to greet her father properly and the unfamiliarity of this new, Parisian version of him. Sensing her hesitation, Derek stood and embraced her, planting not one, not two, but three kisses on her cheeks in true French fashion.

As they sat, Mary studied her father more closely. Gone was the slightly dishevelled, cardigan-wearing man she knew. In his place sat someone... dapper. He'd lost weight, and was that a new shirt? The transformation was startling.

Derek raised his hand, catching the attention of a passing waitress. 'What would you like to drink?' he asked Mary.

'A cappuccino, please?'

Derek's eyebrow arched. 'If you must. But you realise that's an Italian drink, don't you?'

Mary's jaw dropped slightly. 'Since when did you care about things like that?'

'I don't particularly care, just mentioning it in case you want a French coffee.'

'No thanks – cappuccino for me.'

As her father ordered the coffees in flawless French, Mary watched, astounded. The words rolled off his tongue like he'd been speaking the language all his life, not struggling with 'merci' and 'au revoir' like he usually did on their family holidays to Brittany.

'Have you had a stroke or something?' The words burst out of Mary before she could stop them.

Derek's brow furrowed. 'Of course not; why would you ask that?'

Mary leaned forward, her voice low. 'You know how some people have strokes, or they get a bump on their head, and they wake up, and they can only speak Chinese? It's like you had a stroke, woke up, and now you're a dapper Frenchman. Do you have a stripey t-shirt and a string of onions in your bag?'

'Are you suggesting I wasn't dapper before?' Derek asked, a hint of amusement in his voice.

Mary couldn't help but laugh. 'You weren't at all dapper. What's the opposite of dapper? You were that. You were minus on the dapper scale.'

'Very funny, Mary.'

'How do you say that in French?'

'Très amusant,' Derek replied without missing a beat.

'Christ,' Mary muttered, shaking her head in disbelief.

As they sipped their coffee—the rich and frothy cappuccino a stark contrast to the bitter espresso Derek had chosen—Mary found herself studying her father. The Derek Brown sitting across from her seemed years younger than the man she'd left behind in England. His eyes sparkled with a vitality she couldn't remember seeing before, and there was an ease to his movements that spoke of a newfound confidence.

'So,' Mary began, desperate to understand this transformation, 'when did you become Monsieur Sophistiqué? Last I checked, your idea of international cuisine was ordering chips at the local Chinese takeaway.'

Derek chuckled, the sound warm and genuine. 'People can change, you know. Your mother always said I needed to broaden my horizons.'

At the mention of her mother, Mary felt a twinge of unease. There was something in her father's tone, a note of... what? Sadness? Regret? She couldn't quite place it.

'Speaking of Mum,' Mary said, reaching into her bag, 'she asked me to give you this.' She pulled out the envelope Rosie had entrusted to her, sliding it across the table.

Derek's eyes flickered with an unreadable emotion as he took the envelope, tucking it into his jacket pocket without opening it. 'I'll read it later,' he said softly.

The moment stretched between them, heavy with unspoken words. Mary wondered what secrets that envelope might hold, what silent conversation her parents were having.

As they finished their coffees and prepared to leave the station, Mary attempted to fill the silence with stories of her and Rosie's Parisian adventures. She edited as she went, trying to paint a picture of a sophisticated mother-daughter trip rather than the chaotic, often hilarious reality.

'...and then we visited the Louvre,' Mary said as they stepped onto the Metro, the doors hissing closed behind them. She carefully omitted the part about accidentally stumbling into a secret room full of humanoid robots. 'The Mona Lisa is smaller than you'd think.'

Derek nodded, a knowing smile playing on his lips. 'And did you and your mother behave yourselves? No causing international incidents?'

Mary laughed, perhaps a touch too loudly. 'Us? Never. We're the picture of decorum.'

Mary studied her father's reflection in the window as the Metro rattled through the tunnels beneath Paris. Who was this man? The Derek Brown she knew would never have hopped on a train to Paris alone, let alone seemed so at ease in a foreign city. Yet here he was, navigating the Metro like a local, peppering his speech with French phrases as if he'd been bilingual since childhood.

The pieces didn't fit, and Mary couldn't shake the feeling that there was more to this story than met the eye. What was in that envelope from her mother? Why had her father really come to Paris? And most importantly, what did all of this mean for their family?

As they emerged from the Metro station into the late afternoon sunshine, Paris sprawled before them in all its glory. The Eiffel Tower loomed in the distance. Mary took a deep breath, inhaling the scents of the city – fresh bread, coffee, and that indefinable essence that was purely Paris.

'Well,' Derek said, clapping his hands, 'shall we head to the hotel? I'm sure your mother is waiting for us.'

'Yes, but shouldn't you read the note before we get back. Mum was very insistent that I give it to you.'

'Oh, yeah, sure,' he said, putting down his bag and retrieving the letter from his pocket. He glanced through it, thrust it back into his pocket and shook his head in disgust.

'This is a disaster,' he said,

'What is?'

'Your mother asked us to get some shopping for her while we're out.'

'That's OK. We can do that.'

'Yes, but for pants. Women's pants.'

The look on her father's face was one of such confusion and concern that Mary reached over and hugged him. 'What's happened to the confident Parisian? Come on, Dad, you can do it.'

'You'll have to get them.'

'I'm not getting them. She left the note for you.'

The thought of watching her middle-aged father trouping through the lingerie section at a French store was too glorious to interfere with. Where was the fun in Mary buying them?

It turned out that there were very strict and detailed instructions about the kind of knickers he was to buy. In addition to written instructions spelling out exactly what colour, size, and fabric she wanted, Mrs Brown had pushed a pair of the target knickers into the envelope to act as a template, or perhaps like one of those Dulux colour charts. Mary watched her father walk slowly towards the knicker section in the harsh light of the department store.

He'd lost some of his earlier confidence in the face of such a monumental task, but Mary remained impressed (and confused) by how smart he looked. Usually, he'd be dressed in a sweatshirt, which pre-dated her birth. It would be smudged and grimed by age and chilli sauce and paired with trousers that looked like they'd been shot out of a cannon during the dying stages of a siege when all other ammunition had been exhausted.

Her father pulled the knickers out of the envelope with tangible reluctance. He then held them up against other garments on the racks, eager to see whether they were a match. He shook his head and looked around in search of his daughter.

But Mary was committed to being no help at all. She wouldn't permit herself to be associated with the mission. Realising his daughter was nowhere to be seen, he reached out to a higher authority, recruiting a shop assistant to help him in his quest.

From her position, crouching behind the bras, Mary watched her father laughing and conversing with the woman in his newly acquired French.

Then he did something Mary never thought she'd see: He took the pants proffered by the assistant and held them against his pelvis area as if checking them for size and cut. He did a small wiggle, which seemed to greatly amuse the lady, and he thanked her and headed over to the till with them.

'Well done,' said Mary, sneaking up behind him.

'I found someone to help me,' he admitted.

'I know. I saw. She seemed very taken with you.'

Derek Brown smiled. 'Fancy lunch,' he said.

'Sure. But shouldn't we go and find Mum and see whether she fancies coming?'

'No, we'll catch up with her afterwards. There's something I want to tell you first.'

The couple left the store after Derek had stuffed the bag containing the embarrassing garments deep into his jacket pocket.

When they sat down, he was still shaking his head at knickergate, and Mary was still shaking her head at the image of her father holding up frilly knickers in front of him while a flirty Parisian shop worker watched him.

Mary ordered a salad, feeling the need to eat something a little healthier after all the gorging of the past couple of days. Her father ordered croque monsieur.

'A little glass of wine?' he suggested.

'Just water for me, thanks.'

They clinked their glasses together.

'To a lovely few days in Paris,' said Mary.

Derek smiled at her in a half-hearted fashion.

The food arrived, and they ate in silence. As soon as Mary had finished, Derk took her hands and looked deep into her eyes.

'Your mother's leaving me,' he said.

'What?'

'Yes. Don't tell her I told you…she wants to tell you herself, but she's going - she doesn't want to be with me anymore.'

'What? What are you talking about? Is this because of the knickers or something? I don't understand.'

'No, sweetheart. Nothing to do with that.'

Mary looked at her father's face. Suddenly, he looked older and more vulnerable than he'd ever looked before.

'What did you say, Dad? I think I misheard you.'

'Rosie is leaving me.'

Four little words and Mary's world spun on its axis.

CHAPTER 14: SHATTERED FOUNDATIONS

Mary sat in the hotel reception, looking around angrily. Her mother had gone to get the coffees while Mary contemplated the conversation ahead. She'd texted her mun straight after the chat with her dad.

'Can you meet me at the café in reception, mum? We need to talk. '

'Of course,' her mun had replied.

So, here she was, waiting for her mum to return, and the longer Rosie took to order two coffees, the angrier Mary was getting.

She couldn't believe this was happening. And for her to hear about it here…in Paris, of all places. The city of love. Ha! Not to her, it wasn't. More like the city of unravelling dreams and crushing disappointment.

How could her parents split up? What was the point? What was her mother thinking? Surely she wasn't planning on meeting someone else at her age, was she? Christ, she was nearly 60. 60!

There was a greater chance of her being hit by a bus than

of meeting a man interested in dating a woman on a fast track to a pension book.

Her mother needed to grow up.

Dad was a lovely man. He had his faults, as everyone did, and yes – sure, he could do with losing a bit of weight and doing a bit more around the house, but he was decent, honourable and– most importantly - the two of them had stood up in church a million years ago and promised to stay with each other forever. Additionally, they had a daughter for whom they needed to stay together. Perhaps Mary didn't count. Perhaps her mother had become so selfish that she didn't even think how it would affect her only child. Mary felt wretched.

Her parents had always been there for her, this immovable force sitting valiantly between her and all her problems. She'd turned to them whenever she felt sad, lost, or confused. They were her bridge over troubled waters, her calm in a storm, her greatest allies, and her warmest companions.

Not now, they weren't, with Dad forced to move out and live in a bus shelter somewhere, living off bird food, and Mum too busy going on internet dates.

Christ, the future did not look bright at all.

Derek had asked Mary not to tell her mum or mention that she knew about their impending divorce. He said she should wait for her mum to bring it up. This put Mary in an unenviable position. Mary wasn't prepared to sit there making small talk when she knew what horrible secret her mother was harbouring and what plans she had for her grubby life post-divorce.

She'd told her father she would try to persuade her mum to tell her, but Mary would bring it up herself if Rosie didn't mention it.

While Mary had headed off to meet Rosie, Derek had gone to check-in.

Now she watched as her mother headed back towards her. Christ, what if her mum had already met someone? Mary hadn't considered that before, but what if Rosie had taken a lover? Some grubby Italian waiter with a ridiculously long pepper grinder and offensively tight trousers. What then? How would that work? How would Mary be introduced to him? 'Hey. Here's your new daddy. He was three years behind you in school.'

For God's Sake - her mother was too old for all this nonsense.

Mary wasn't having any of it. She wasn't interested in meeting any new man her mother might've met. She didn't want any ne'er-do-wells trooping through the house. She had a father, thank you very much.

'Coffees are on the way,' said Rosie. She noticed Mary was deep in thought.

'Penny for them,' she said, touching her daughter lightly on the shoulder.

Mary knew she couldn't mention anything, so instead, she tried to prompt her mother to talk about it.

'I spoke to Dad when I picked him up earlier; he seemed quiet, not himself,' said Mary.

'Yes, he's not quite himself at the moment,' said Rosie.

'It's more than that, though, isn't it?' said Mary, fiddling with the cutlery on the table, moving the sugar sachets around and doing everything she could to avoid looking at her mother. 'I know something is wrong: why can't you just tell me what it is? Has he had very bad news from the doctor or something?'

'He's got a few medical issues. He hasn't looked after himself...you know what men can be like. He's been eating too much, drinking too much, and taking no exercise whatsoever for years. He's been much better recently, but he needs to do more exercise. I've told him to come with me when I take your Elvis for a walk, but he's not interested. He'd rather sit at home drinking beer. He needs to take his medication, eat more healthily and exercise more…that's all there is to it.'

'I thought he looked well. He seemed healthier and happier than he has in ages. But he's ill, is he?'

'Yes.'

'What's wrong with him? Tell me the truth.'

Mary could feel her heart beating in her chest.

'I am telling you the truth. He's not been well, but he'll be fine if he takes his health seriously.'

'So, why does it feel like such doom and gloom? Why do I feel that you are keeping something from me? I thought we were close, Mum, but this feels awful.'

'Oh angel, I'm sorry, I'm sorry, I'm sorry. There is something I want to say. I've wanted to tell you for days but couldn't bring myself to.'

'Try now, mum.'

'Your father and I are splitting up. We're not getting divorced yet, but he will be moving out.'

'So, basically - you're leaving him when he's ill.'

'No, I'm not - he's not ill.'

'You said he was.'

'He has pre-diabetes and high blood pressure. To be fair to him – he's addressing it. He's lost some weight and is taking it seriously. But it's not an illness.'

'It's not an illness? What are you talking about? People die from that. High blood pressure can kill.'

'He'll be fine. He's a tough man, your dad.'

'I can't believe this. Your callousness knows no bounds. I don't understand why you're behaving like this.'

'Like what, sweetheart?'

'DON'T call me sweetheart. You are such a cow.'

Mary pushed her chair back so it scraped across the floor, emitting a screech as it dragged along.

Haughty Parisiennes glanced around as Mary stood up, grabbed her bag, and ran out of the reception, into the street outside. She ran as fast as she could until completely out of sight.

She could feel her bag vibrating as her phone rang. It was bound to be her mother, of course. But what did her mother think she could say to make everything OK again?

Mary dipped into a side street, out of sight, and checked her phone. The call was from an unknown number.

'Hello, is it Mary?' came a friendly voice.

'Yes, who is this?'

'Ah, it's Wayne from Hampton Court Pizzas. Just checking you're OK.'

'I'm OK?'

'Yes, you haven't ordered pizza in a while. We wanted to make sure everything was OK.'

Christ, did she order pizza that often?

'I'm OK.'

'You sound sad.'

'Well, yes if you must know, my life is completely falling apart. I'm having a nightmare of epic proportions.

'You want pizza?'

'No – I don't want pizza.'

'Pizza makes everything better. We give you half price for being such a loyal customer.'

'No – I don't want any pizza. Please don't call again.'

TED STARED into the toilet as if he were staring into the eyes of a lover. Then he stood up abruptly, knocking his head sharply on the large screw protruding from the side of the porcelain.

'Shit.'

He moved away from the toilet and kicked the pile of tools laid out on a towel in front of him. Why was this so hard? Why did he struggle so much to do the most basic of tasks? The toilet seat had been wobbly for about a year, and he knew how much it annoyed Mary. He'd avoided fixing it thus far by leaving the room every time she complained, but he decided he would mend it while she was in Paris. After all, given the news she'd had, this was the least he could do.

He picked up the diagram again and studied it intently. Why was it so hard to understand what any of it meant? Most men appeared to be able to look at instructions and understand what they meant, but not him. The task seemed utterly beyond his capabilities. Where did he even begin? How the seat connected to the pan looked like it would need the sort of engineering skills indistinguishable from magic.

He had already tried and failed several times that morning, despite watching several YouTube videos in which competent men in overalls fixed loose toilet seats with strong-fingered ease. But none of the seating technologies seemed quite the same as the one he was looking at. He opened the iPad again and watched another video. Then, full of renewed confidence, he went to the bathroom, stared at the lavatory for a while, jabbed at it randomly with an inappropriate tool, then returned to the screen and began the cycle again.

It took him about 20 minutes of searching until - finally - he saw a video featuring a toilet seat not unlike his own. He tried again. He removed the screw he'd attempted to force into a tiny hole and freed the seat and lid with a sharp jerk. Then he placed the new one over the toilet and began banging, screwing and pushing; force and skill united in a graceful ballet. The screws were tightened. The seat was restored. It felt like the completion of some quest in an epic fantasy series. He'd never felt this competent or, to be frank, manly.

He stood back and admired his work.

Maybe your average man would consider this a simple task, but not him - this was a magnificent achievement, and he would rest in the afterglow of contentment that swept over him. He moved forward and lifted the toilet seat, then dropped it again - it returned to its position slowly and without banging on the lavatory.

What a classy piece of work.

TED HEARD his phone ring in his jeans pocket and pulled it out. Whoever was on the end of this phone would hear all about his remarkable achievement regardless of the reason for their call.

Happily, it was Mary's name which flashed on the screen.

'You won't believe what I've just done..." he said to his wife, barely able to contain his excitement.

'What you've done? What do you mean?'

'I mended the toilet seat at last. I did it all myself. I found a video on YouTube and tried to copy it, but it turned out to be a different seat, so I went back onto YouTube and I...'

'Why are you talking about toilet seats when my life has collapsed?'

'What do you mean - your life has collapsed?'

'Mum's leaving Dad.'

'No, she's not.

'Yes, she is. My dad just told me. They are supposed to be my parents. Why are they acting like such children?'

'I don't know love. Did your mum say why she's leaving?'

'Because she's a bitch.'

'Wooah, Mary. I'm sure there's a sensible reason. You

need to talk to her and find out what's going on. People grow apart, you know.'

'I know, but not parents - they have no right to go around splitting up when they've got a child.'

'You're not a child. You're a grown woman...you're married. You need to be the person who steps up and looks after your parents now, just as your parents have supported you for all these years. It may be that your parents need you to be a grown-up right now.'

Mary sat in silence.

'Can you hear me?' asked Ted.

'Of course, I can hear you.'

'Am I making sense?'

'I'm heartbroken, Ted. The last thing I need is bloody commonsense.'

'Listen to me, angel. Go and find your mum, take her out for a glass of wine or a coffee or something, and check she's OK.'

'Check, she's OK. Oh, I'm sure she's fine. It's Dad I'm worried about. Christ, how could she leave him? They are old. I bet she's met someone else. I bet she has.'

'I don't know, Mary, and neither will you unless you talk to her properly. Have you spoken to her at all since your dad told you?'

'Only briefly, but I ran out of the hotel before she could finish talking to me.'

'Go and talk to her, and call me back.'

'OK,' said Mary, weakly.

CHAPTER 15: SUSPICIONS AND SILENCES

Ted looked down at his handwork once again. No one could say that was anything but a first-class job. Perhaps he should retire from sales and set up his own handyman business.

He'd contemplate that prospect over the coming days.

For now, though, he had a distressed wife to worry about. Could Rosie and Derek be splitting up? It seemed unfeasible. Not because they were the perfect couple by any means, but because they were old. They might as well keep going and live separate lives if necessary.

Ted thought about the situation a little more. Perhaps Rosie was having an affair. That would explain why a separation was vital. Rosie had met someone new and wanted to pursue a life with him.

Mary's mum had always seemed so much more glamorous than her husband. She was eager to go out and meet people and generally more sociable than the 'stay-at-home' Derek. Perhaps it was a toy boy? The thought seemed ridiculous, but the thought of Mary's salt-of-the-earth parents deciding to separate was ridiculous in itself.

WE'LL ALWAYS HAVE PARIS

He pondered the awfulness of her parents separating and Rosie moving in with a man the same age as Mary. Perhaps it was someone they knew?

Mary would be devastated. The stress of all this was too much for her. Ted needed to get to Paris to find out what was happening and look after his wife. He pulled out his phone to look at train times and then phoned the office to tell them he needed a few days off.

It would be a nice surprise for her. He'd buy some beautiful flowers and take her out to the best restaurant in Paris, and he'd look after her. This was perfect.

Ted went onto Google and typed: 'romantic things to do in Paris.' They'd have a ball. He read about breakfast at Les Deux Magots, champagne atop the Eiffel tour, walking in Montmartre, and maybe a river cruise down the Seine.

He was going to Paris.

MARY LOOKED out across the Paris Street. Suddenly, the place didn't seem so glitzy and gorgeous. The afternoon felt empty and flat after a gentle morning that held so much promise. She tried to entertain herself by watching people buzzing around, but she couldn't even see any glamorous outfits to admire.

Then she saw her mum walking down the street...strutting along as if on the catwalk: a fabulous silk navy shirt, white trousers, sunglasses and a red handbag that Mary had never seen before.

Where was she going?

Mary had the distinct impression that her mum was up to no good, and she knew what she must do. The afternoon suddenly had a purpose. She slipped out from the small alleyway she'd slunk into and threw herself into a full-scale stalking mission.

Her heart pounded as she half ran, half jogged up the street towards where Rosie had been walking. It took her a while of speedy walking before she caught sight of her mother. Rosie was moving at such speed that she was difficult to keep up with. Then, a flash of red handbag indicated that Rosie had descended the steps into the Metro.

Mary would creep down the steps after her, then get into a different carriage and tuck herself away so she couldn't be seen; what could go wrong?

Her mother seemed to be taking the metro to the shopping area of town, so she was up to - buying new clothes to wear when she was out with her fancy man.

Rosie stepped into one carriage and Mary into another. It meant she had to keep her eyes peeled for her mother's exit from the train.

As they came into the train station for the Champs Elysees, Mary stood by the door, looking out.

People milled around, but there was no sight of her mother. There were adults, children, old people and – there!

Rosie came mincing down the platform with her handbag hanging from the crook of her arm.

'Target, in sight, target in sight,' said Mary, as if talking into a tiny microphone. She was in full-flight detective mode as she walked along the platform, keeping a safe distance, ducking behind pillars and diving into crevices when necessary.

She could teach Interpol a thing or two.

Her mother jogged up the steps. That hadn't been in the plan. How was her mum so fit? Mary ran after her, fervently hoping for less jogging as the pursuit continued.

Once she reached the top of the steps, she ran out after her mother, stopping abruptly as she saw Rosie pause to answer her phone.

Mary was in a quandary now.

Should she attempt to listen to the phone call?

It could be from one of her mother's fancy men.

Or should she stay back, wait for her to finish, and continue to follow her?

It was the sort of dilemma that every Secret Service agent faced. Unusually, Mary opted for the sensible option and stayed back out of sight until her mother resumed her walk, at which point she followed her from a distance. She guessed her mother was heading for Galleries Lafayette, the glamorous department store with a million shops. It was where the two of them had been heading when the badger and right-wing march collided to prevent them.

Her mother was obviously heading off to buy fantastically gorgeous clothes for her lover.

Rosie turned and walked into a makeup and perfume shop and tried to concentrate on choosing a lipstick that her daughter would like. There wasn't a great deal she could do about Mary's upset, but if she could get her the beautiful red lipstick that she wanted, it might put a smile on her face.

The trouble was—there were so many red lipsticks, from coral to cherry red, scarlet to an almost bluey red, and a deep, dark shade of burgundy. She thought about her daughter's colouring...perhaps the coral shade?

'This one, please,' she said to the assistant.

Mary watched carefully, trying to work out what her mother had bought.

It seemed like some makeup, perhaps some false eyelashes, to make her look young and flirty. This wasn't a pleasant scene for a daughter to witness.

Not a pleasant scene at all.

MARY WALKED AWAY and decided she needed to eat. Although she had done nothing but eat since arriving, food was so comforting, and she felt like she deserved it after everything she'd been through.

She slid onto the worn leather banquette of a small bistro near the hotel. The place hummed with quiet conversation, starkly contrasting the chaos in her mind. She absently traced the red-and-white checked tablecloth, her eyes unfocused.

A waiter approached. 'Bonsoir, mademoiselle. Le menu?'

Mary nodded, accepting the card without really seeing it. As she pretended to study the offerings, her phone buzzed. Rosie's name flashed on the screen. Mary's thumb hovered over the green button before decisively hitting 'decline.'

She set the phone face-down as it lit up with a text: 'Darling, let's have dinner together. We need to talk.'

Mary's jaw clenched. She flagged down the waiter. 'Burger and fries, s'il vous plaís.'

Across town, Rosie lowered her phone, her reflection in the restaurant window showing the flicker of hope dying in her eyes. The maître d' approached. 'Madame? Your table is ready.'

Rosie followed him to a small table for two, painfully aware of the empty chair across from her. She ordered a glass of Bordeaux, leaving the menu untouched.

As the waiter retreated, Rosie's gaze fell on a young couple at a nearby table. The woman laughed, reaching across to touch her partner's hand. Rosie's hand twitched, remembering countless dinners with Derek. She blinked rapidly, turning to stare out the window at the twinkling Parisian night.

Meanwhile, in a sleek, modern restaurant, Derek adjusted his tie, feeling it suddenly too tight. The maître d' led him to a prime table with a view of the Eiffel Tower. Any other night, he'd have revelled in the exclusivity. Tonight, the opulence felt hollow. His wife had said she wanted to be left alone, and his daughter wasn't talking to him, and he knew it was all his own fault.

'Monsieur, may I recommend our chef's tasting menu?'

Derek nodded absently, his mind replaying Mary's face as he'd told her about the divorce. The hurt, the betrayal in her eyes. He'd let her believe it was Rosie's idea, a coward's move.

Now, as he sat alone in this temple to haute cuisine, the guilt gnawed at him.

Back at the bistro, Mary pushed her fries around the plate. The garlic butter, usually a favourite, turned her stomach. She took a large bite of her burger, wincing at its cloying taste.

A burst of laughter from a nearby table made her flinch. A family—mother, father, daughter—shared a joke over their meal. Mary's hand tightened on her cutlery. She pulled out her phone, thumb hovering over Rosie's number before she put the phone down. Then she texted her parents, 'I need to be alone tonight. I hope you understand.'

Rosie sat motionless, her wine untouched. The waiter had long since given up on taking her order. She stared at her phone, willing it to ring. Each passing minute felt like a rejection, confirming Mary's anger. She knew she should eat, but the thought of food turned her stomach. Instead, she took a small sip of wine, barely tasting it.

As she laid her glass back down, she saw the text on her phone. Mary was clearly upset, but Rosie felt incredibly unfair that her daughter was blaming her. Rosie didn't want her marriage to end any more than Mary did.

In the high-end restaurant, Derek cut into his perfectly cooked steak, the knife slicing through without resistance. He chewed mechanically, the rich flavour lost on him. His eyes drifted to his phone, half hoping for a message from Rosie or Mary, half dreading what they might say.

As the evening wore on, the three sat in their separate

restaurants, each lost in their own thoughts. Mary, nursing her resentment and confusion. Rosie, awash with sadness and longing for her daughter.

Derek, marinating in guilt and indecision, looked down at the message. He'd hurt his daughter and lied to her. It was unforgivable.

The City of Light sparkled outside their windows, oblivious to the family fracturing within its embrace.

CHAPTER 16: AFTER THE STORM: COMFORT INBOUND

In England, the situation was considerably less tense. Ted sat back on the sofa and folded his arms behind his head. Now that he was ready to go to Paris, he was looking forward to it. He loved that he'd be able to surprise Mary, spend time with her and be there for Rosie's birthday dinner. He was sure that she'd misunderstood the situation with her parents. Rosie and Derek were a great couple. They weren't splitting up – it was all in Mary's mind.

He got up, switched off the television and walked into the bedroom, shoved his clothes into his case in a manner which he knew would annoy his wife.stuffing it in rather than folding it neatly.

Then he checked once again that he had his passport and his Eurostar ticket

ROSIE BROWN'S heels clicked against the parquet floor as she entered her Parisian-style room, the sound echoing in the empty space. She paused before the elegant, full-length mirror, its distressed frame a beautiful counterpoint to the shabby chic furniture surrounding her. A magnificent chandelier cast a soft glow, its crystals tinkling gently in the breeze from the open window.

Her reflection stared back, a stranger in familiar skin. Rosie leaned closer, her manicured nails tracing the lines etched around her eyes. The kohl pencil she'd so carefully applied now seemed to emphasize every crease, every sign of the years she'd lived. Her crimson lips, once bold and defiant, now appeared garish in the muted light.

She fingered the glamorous earrings adorning her lobes, their weight suddenly oppressive. A mirthless chuckle escaped her throat. Who was she trying to fool? This carefully constructed facade wasn't her, not really. Not anymore.

Rosie's mind drifted to the Parisian streets she'd navigated earlier, her ankles wobbling precariously on heels she once would have considered sensible. The memory of French men tipping their caps as she passed now felt like a mockery rather than a compliment.

She shuddered, grateful she'd resisted Suzy's insistence on the full-length faux fur coat. That would have been the final touch in this caricature of herself she'd created.

Rosie's gaze locked onto her reflection once more, zeroing in on the strands of grey peeking through her carefully maintained color. When had that happened? It seemed like only yesterday she was...

The thought trailed off as a new, more painful one took its place. Why now? Why, just as the signs of age were becoming impossible to ignore, did he choose to leave? And for a younger woman, no less. The cliché of it all burned like acid in her throat.

She sank onto the edge of her bed, the Marie Antoinette-inspired spread cool beneath her palms. The room that had once felt so right now seemed to mock her with its youthful elegance.

Rosie's hand moved unconsciously to her neck, massaging a knot that had taken up permanent residence. When had simple movements become such a challenge? The click of her knee as she crossed her legs sounded obscenely loud in the quiet room.

Her gaze drifted to her vanity, littered with creams and serums that promised miracles but delivered only disappointment. And her hair - oh, her hair. Once her crowning glory, it now resembled nothing so much as a abandoned bird's nest each morning, dry and unmanageable.

As she stared at her reflection, the reality of her situation crashed over her like a wave. Not only was she facing the indignities of ageing, but she was doing so alone. The prospect of starting over loomed before her, a mountain she wasn't sure she had the strength to climb.

How does one date at this age? How does one learn to be alone after decades of partnership? The questions swirled in her mind, each one more daunting than the last.

Rosie's eyes landed on a magazine left open on her nightstand, its glossy pages showcasing an array of wigs. For a moment, she allowed herself to imagine it - waking up, showering, and simply donning a perfectly styled wig. No more battles with thinning, listless locks. No more gasping at the ever-widening part that refused to be concealed.

She shook her head, dispelling the fantasy. This was her reality now - ageing, alone, starting from scratch. The woman in the mirror might be a stranger, but she was all Rosie had. Somehow, she would have to find a way forward, one wobbly step at a time.

She picked up the phone to ring Pauline, but the answerphone clicked in straight away. She called her sister instead… Susan would know what to do.

'How's it going?' said Susan.

'It's OK,' said Rosie, bursting into tears. But Derek isn't

talking to me. We almost got arrested in The Louvre. I accidentally went on a right-wing march, and I did the can-can on stage.'

'OK...'

'Why do these sorts of things always happen to me?'

'They could happen to anyone,' said Susan, trying to mollify her distressed sister. 'The number of times I've gone to Tesco's and accidentally done the can-can at a cabaret club then encountered a right-wing march in the frozen veg section. Happens all the time.'

Rosie laughed.

'I'm coming out to see you. I want to be there on your birthday,' said Susan. 'I'll come on Sunday. How about that?'

CHAPTER 17: ARRIVALS AND DEPARTURES

SATURDAY

Rosie's night was a restless tapestry of half-formed dreams and sudden awakenings. As dawn broke, she found herself still ensnared in a fog of fatigue. She'd neglected to draw the curtains, allowing the morning sun to pierce through the window and dazzle her weary face.

Despite her exhaustion, a flicker of joy ignited within her at the thought of Susan's impending arrival. Perhaps her sister could bridge the chasm that had formed between Rosie and Mary. With Susan there, the burden of explanations, apologies, and reassurances might ease from Rosie's shoulders, if only slightly.

A gentle chime from her phone heralded a text from Sue, confirming her journey and offering words of comfort: 'Don't fret, Rosie. Just be honest with Mary...that's all you need to do. She's a grown woman, after all.'

Rosie's lips curved into a wistful smile at those last words. The concept of Mary as a 'grown woman' seemed almost comically absurd, a notion her maternal heart struggled to reconcile. In Rosie's eyes, Mary would forever remain her little girl - the child with unruly pigtails, always a touch more dishevelled than her peers, with a mischievous glint in her eye that outshone them all. She was the girl whose wit sparkled brighter, whose laughter rang clearer, and whose beauty, to Rosie at least, eclipsed that of every other child.

As the sun climbed higher, bathing the room in a warm glow, Rosie found herself caught between the pressing realities of the present and the cherished memories of the past. The day ahead loomed with its challenges, but for a moment, Rosie allowed herself to linger in the comforting embrace of a past world in which her daughter would always be that endearing, slightly scruffy little girl with the world at her feet.

She pictured Mary at six, her tiny frame poised on the balance beam, tongue peeking out in concentration as she executed a perfect cartwheel. The same day, she'd found Mary hanging upside down from a tree in the backyard, leaves tangled in her unruly pigtails, a mischievous grin plastered across her face.

Then there was the time Mary decided to 'redecorate' the living room. Rosie had stepped out for ten minutes to chat with a neighbour, only to return to a sea of crayon masterpieces adorning the cream wallpaper. Mary stood in the centre, beaming with pride, her hands and face a rainbow of waxy colours.

At eight, Mary's gymnastics coach had praised her natural talent, right before Mary used that same talent to scale the school building and rescue a kite stuck on the roof. The headmistress's face was a picture of conflicting emotions— impressed by the feat yet exasperated by the breach of rules.

Rosie smiled as she thought back to the science fair debacle. Twelve-year-old Mary, determined to win first prize, had created a 'volcanic eruption' that was too realistic. This resulted in the classroom being evacuated and the fire department being summoned. Yet somehow, covered in foam and grinning from ear to ear, Mary had charmed the judges into awarding her the blue ribbon.

Rosie's reverie was interrupted by a chuckle. She realised she was grinning, her cheeks aching from the memories. Mary had been a handful - energetic, willful, and endlessly curious. But she'd also been a joy, filling their home with laughter, surprises, and more love than Rosie had ever thought possible.

Her little whirlwind was all grown up now, facing adult problems. Yet a part of Rosie couldn't help but hope that somewhere inside the woman Mary had become, that mischievous, bright-eyed little girl still lived on, ready to face the world with the same fearless spirit she'd always had.

She knew she needed to talk to her daughter.

'Mary, it's me. Can you come to my room? We need to talk. Let's deal with this like adults. Stop ignoring me.'

Mary had seen her mother's number appear on the phone's screen but had chosen not to answer. She played the message and felt a stab of anger. If her mum wanted to have this out, they would have this out.

She knocked on the door of her mum's room and burst into it as soon as Rosie opened it a fraction.

'Come on then, mum. Let's talk,' Mary said, her voice sharp.

Rosie closed the door softly, her hand lingering on the handle as she steeled herself. She turned to face her daughter, pacing the room like a caged tiger.

Mary's eyes darted around, taking in the surroundings. Her gaze landed on a recent picture of Mary, Derek and Rosie that her mum had obviously brought with her. Mary's jaw clenched.

'How could you do this? After all these years, you're just... what? Bored? Tired of being a wife and mother?'

Rosie opened her mouth to speak, but Mary cut her off with a sharp gesture.

'No, let me finish. I thought we were happy. I thought *you* were happy.'

Mary's voice cracked slightly. She ran a hand through her hair, disheveling it.

'Was it all a lie? Every family dinner, every holiday, every time you told Dad you loved him?'

Rosie took a step towards her daughter, her hand outstretched. 'Mary, please, if you'd just let me explain.'

Mary recoiled as if Rosie's touch would burn her. 'Explain what? How you are throwing away thirty years of marriage? How you are destroying our family?'

Tears welled in Rosie's eyes, but she blinked them back. 'It's not that simple, darling. There are things you don't understand.'

'Then make me understand!' Mary shouted, her composure finally cracking. 'Because from where I'm standing, it looks like you're walking out on Dad, me, and everything we've built together.'

Rosie sank onto the sofa, her shoulders sagging under the weight of her daughter's accusations. 'Mary, please, sit down. This isn't easy for any of us.'

Mary remained standing, her arms crossed tightly over her chest. 'No, I don't want to sit down. I want answers. Why now? Why like this?'

Rosie looked up at her daughter, seeing not the angry woman before her but the little girl who used to climb into her lap for comfort.

'Your father and I...' Rosie began, her voice barely above a whisper. 'We've been having problems for a while now. We tried to keep it from you, to work things out ourselves.'

Mary scoffed. 'Problems? Everyone has problems. You work through them. You don't just give up.'

'I'm not giving up!' Rosie's voice rose, surprising them both. She took a deep breath. 'Mary, things are happening that you don't know about, and they can't be fixed by just trying harder.'

'Then tell me!' Mary's voice was raw with frustration. 'Stop hiding behind vague excuses and just tell me the truth!'

Rosie stood up suddenly, her frustration finally boiling over. 'You want the truth? Fine. IT'S NOT ME WHO'S LEAVING. YOUR FATHER IS HAVING AN AFFAIR!'

The words hung in the air between them, heavy and irrevocable. Mary staggered back as if physically struck, her face draining of colour.

'What?' she whispered, her anger evaporating, replaced by shock and disbelief.

Rosie's shoulders slumped, the fight going out of her. 'Your father... he's been seeing someone else. I know he has. He won't talk about it or admit it, but I know. I just KNOW. He wants to leave. He wants a divorce. It's not me. I still love him.'

'But, dad said...' Mary's words faded from her. This was too much to deal with.

'I'm going home. This is the worst week of my life,' said Mary, leaving the room and walking down the long corridor.

TED'S TRAIN arrived at Gare du Nord, and he gathered his overnight bag and coat together and stepped off onto the platform. He planned to buy his wife an enormous bouquet of red roses and a bottle of French champagne; then, he'd book a table for lunch at the most Parisian place he could find. He might have frogs' legs, he'd definitely have garlic. Hell - he might even buy a beret and sport it nattily on the side of his head. He was in Paris, for goodness' sake. Anything could happen.

'Bonjour, she suis en Paris. See vous tres soon,' he typed into WhatsApp. 'I am heading towards the hotel. Love you xx'

MARY DIDN'T NOTICE the message coming through on her phone. To be honest, an elephant could have walked into the train carriage, and she wouldn't have noticed. She was miles away, thinking of her parents splitting up, and wondering what on earth that meant for the future.

But while she felt sorry for herself, she also felt a pang of regret at how she had treated her mother. She'd assumed it had been Rosie who had betrayed the marriage. Hadn't her father as much as said it was her mum's fault? She felt a new wave of anger towards her dad, just as the one directed at her mother began to lift.

Christ, the way she'd followed her mum yesterday, determined to find something underhand in her actions. Could her dad really be having an affair? She remembered how great he'd looked at the station, gently puffing on a cigarette without a care.

Did he have a young lover? Was the lover younger than she was? Oh God, it was too horrible to contemplate. Perhaps it was someone she knew? Maybe one of her friends?

Mary tried to shake the image of her dad in his comfy corduroy trousers and wooden jumpers, suddenly going to discos and turning up at the same parties she was at.

Her dad never seemed to want to go anywhere. It was Mum who pushed him to get dressed up and go out. It was Mum who thought they should go to the tennis club, to local theatre productions, and bridge club that they both came to love so much. Without Mum, Dad would be a blob in front of the television, eating bacon sandwiches

WE'LL ALWAYS HAVE PARIS

and Chinese takeaways and refusing the engage with the world.

Why the hell did he want to end the marriage and move out? What had been going on?

She needed to talk to someone... Not her mother or father, but someone who had known her most of her life and knew her parents and would be as shocked as she was by the news. There was only one person: Charlie.

Mary pulled out her phone and rang her friend. She was in a packed train carriage, but she didn't care. She launched into a teary description of what had happened.

'Where are you now?' asked Charlie.

'On the train home.'

'But you need to talk to your parents. Why are you coming home? You need to spend time with them, talk about the whole thing, and discuss the situation.'

Mary was silent, looking down at her hand and teasing the cuticles at the bottom of her thumb. This wasn't the reaction she'd expected.

'Are you still there? What about Ted? I thought he was coming out to Paris. Have you cancelled that now?'

'No, Ted's not coming out to Paris. What are you talking about?'

'Oh. I thought he was. What did your mum say when you told her you were leaving.'

'I just ran off.'

'And your dad?'

'He doesn't know. I just left without saying anything.'

'How can you have just left?'

'I don't need to be cross-examined; I need some support.'

Charlie took a deep breath.

'OK, of course, I'm always here for you. I'll support you all you want; I'm just surprised, that's all. What time does your train get to London? I'll meet you at St Pancras.'

Mary gave Charlie all the information and hung up.

CHAPTER 18: THE PARIS-LONDON DISCONNECT

*osie Brown banged on her daughter's door again. Mary must be in there.

'Please come out, sweetheart. Open the door. I just want to talk to you. We can talk through the door, but chatting face-to-face seems easier. Can you please open it?'

No response.

Rosie phoned her daughter from outside the room and pushed her ear against the door. There was no sound of a ringing phone in the room. No sound of anything. Perhaps she wasn't there? Rosie walked down to reception and asked the receptionist whether she'd seen Mary pass through.

'She leaves earlier. She cancel room.'

DEREK SMILED when he heard a voice on the phone. 'Hey,' he said. 'Sorry, I missed your call. Guess where I am?'

'In bed, naked, waiting for me?' said the loud female voice.

'Nope. I'm in Paris.'

'Oh, so you went then?'

'Yes, I went, and I talked to Mary. I told her that Rosie and I were splitting up. It wasn't easy. She looked devastated.'

'She's a grown-up. She'll get over it.'

'Yes, I know. But it was hard. She looked heartbroken, and all the colour drained from her cheeks.'

'She's lucky that you stayed together for so long. Many kids grow up without their parents. Mine split when I was two. I never had any contact with my father. You've done more than enough. You stayed in that dull marriage for years. It's time for you to have some fun now.'

'It wasn't a dull marriage. That's not fair, Pauline. Rosie is a lovely woman. We've just outgrown one another, that's all.'

'Well, I can't imagine it was a lot of fun. Anyway, let's not talk about her. I'd rather talk about the future, not the past. Are you going to move in here when you move out of your house?'

'Let's talk about it when I get back. I think it would be much kinder to Rosie if I got myself a little flat first, and we could start dating and see how we go.'

'See how we go? We're both putting a bomb under our marriages to see how it goes?'

'Sorry - I didn't mean it like that. I just meant that we have lots of time; let's not rush things. Rosie would find it hard if I moved straight in with you.'

'Well, let's not hurt Rosie. That would be awful.'

'I'm just trying to do something very hurtful in the kindest way possible.'

There was silence on the line.

'Look, I'm going to have to go. Rosie is trying to ring me. She's probably worried about Mary. I better go and talk to her.'

'Okay,' said Pauline. 'Let's not keep Rosie waiting.'

Derek felt a flash of anger that the new woman in his life could be so critical of the wife he'd spent his life with. The woman who had given him a precious daughter and coped with his tantrums over the years, but he let it go.

'I'll see you very soon,' he said, hanging up and answering the phone to Rosie. His wife was sobbing as if her life depended on it. This was all he needed.

'What an earth is the matter?'

'Mary's left, she's gone back to London.'

'No, she hasn't, Ted is arriving today. He sent a text earlier. It's a surprise for her. There's no need to be so dramatic just because she won't answer her phone.'

'I'm not being dramatic at all. She's disappeared. Reception said she left earlier today and cancelled her room.'

'That can't be right. The lady on the reception desk has made a mistake. I'm heading back. I've been for a walk, but I'm only a few minutes away. Why don't I see you in reception in 10 minutes and find out what's going on.'

Rosie sat in the reception area to wait for Derek's arrival. It seemed impossible that Mary had just left. She walked over to the reception desk. A different woman was sitting there now.

'Hello, my daughter was staying in room five, but your colleague told me she moved out this morning. Do you have any information about where she went? '

'The woman scrunched her eyes up as if she didn't quite understand, then picked up the phone and talked in French before putting the phone down and turning back to Rosie.

'I ask my colleague, she says, lady, no say where she goes.'

'What are the nearest hotels to here? Where could she be?' asked Rosie.

'Here is list,' said the receptionist as the large oak doors opened and Derek walked in.

'Has she gone?' he asked. 'Why would you have rushed off like this?'

'I don't know,' said Rosie, close to tears. She knew this

was her fault. It had been she who told Mary that Derek was the one leaving the marriage, which seems to have tipped Mary over the edge.

'I think it's all too much for her,' Rosie said. 'The receptionist gave me this list of local hotels. I guess she could've gone into one of those. Perhaps she just wanted to escape it all for a while.'

'Have you tried ringing her?'

'No, Derek, I never thought of that,' said Rosie sarcastically.

'Okay, okay. I'm just trying to help.'

'You could have helped by not telling our daughter I was breaking up the marriage.'

'What do you mean? I didn't say anything like that. All I said was that we were splitting up. She looked shocked, as you might expect, but seemed perfectly reasonable when she came to terms with it. I had to say something, Rosie. You didn't seem like you were very keen to tell her.'

'When I talked to her about it, she said I was evil for leaving you. It was awful. I had to tell her that it was you who was leaving.'

Derek went quiet.

'She was asking about it, Derek. I don't know what you want me to say, but I had to tell her the truth.'

'Okay, okay. Sure, I understand. Let's try ringing her again now and see if we have any luck.'

They both pulled their phones out...equally keen to be Mary's saviour - the person who could reassure her and urge her to return to the hotel to talk to them.

'I'll call her,' said Derek. 'It's me who needs to reassure her.'

Rosie thought, not for the first time, that she should kick her soon-to-be ex-husband in the groin.

. . .

At Waterloo station, Mary slumped into Charlie's arms. 'What the hell is going on?' she screamed, rather too loudly for Charlie's comfort, given they were in the middle of the train station concourse. People glanced, Mary burst into tears, and Charlie closed her eyes against the disapproving glances of the commuters and travellers around her.

'Come on, let's go home.'

CHAPTER 19: HEARTS REALIGNED

Mary and Charlie sat silently as the train chugged along, passing through Wimbledon on its route to Hampton Court.

'Do you think you better answer the phone?' said Charlie. 'It's been ringing nonstop. I know you don't want to talk to your parents, but at least text them and tell them you're safe.'

Mary pulled her phone from the pockets of her big coat and handed it to Charlie. 'You call them,' she said.

The phone was ringing as Charlie received it. It said 'Dad mobile' on the screen.

'Hello,' said Charlie.

'Oh my God, finally. Where are you? What have you been doing? We've been trying to reach you all morning. We've been so worried.'

'Hello Mr Brown. It's Charlie here. Mary is with me, she is quite safe. Please don't worry.'

'Charlie, I had no idea you were coming to Paris. I'm so glad that she's with you.'

'She's with me, yes. But we're not in Paris. Mary got the

train back this morning. She just needed to get away and think about the situation.'

'What do you mean she's in England? How can she be in England?'

'Like I said - she got the train this morning.'

'Can I talk to her?'

While Charlie asked Mary whether she would be willing to talk to her father, she heard Derek telling Rosie that Mary was in London; Rosie responded with a loud shriek.

'I'm sorry, but Mary doesn't want to talk to anyone. Perhaps I could get her to call you later?'

'Yes, but tell her not to leave it too long. Is she planning to come back to Paris?'

'I don't know. Let me talk to her, and I'll get back to you. I haven't had a chance to chat with her yet, but I promise to call you when I know.'

'Yes, please do, Charlie. And tell her we both love her very much.'

Charlie conveyed Derek's sentiments to Mary and watched as her best friend shrugged off the kind words.

'Do you want me to respond to some of these messages? You've got about 150 of them.'

'Do you whatever you want,' said Mary. She had her forehead up against the train window and stared at the bleak landscape beyond it.

'Oh lord, most of these are from Ted,' said Charlie.

Mary just shrugged.

'I think you need to call him.'

'I'm not calling him. He doesn't care about me; why should I care about him?'

Charlie scanned down through the texts. Mary's lovely husband had travelled out to Paris, secretly, to look after his wife and spend time with her.

The messages ranged from Ted's arrival in Paris to his

standing in reception of the hotel, clutching roses and champagne, to him buying them tickets for a show that afternoon. The messages became increasingly worried as they progressed.

'You have to talk to Ted,' said Charlie.

'I don't have to talk to anyone,' said Mary.

'You know, you're so lucky to have that man. He does everything for you. You have to call him.'

'No, I don't, I'll see him at home.'

'Right, we've been friends for a long time, haven't we?' said Charlie.

'Yes, we have,' said Mary; she knew a lecture was coming.

'Then I can be frank with you?'

'Yes.'

'I think you're behaving appallingly. You should be ashamed of yourself. You have loving parents who adore you. Whether they are together, separate, divorced or married, they will adore you, which is more than enough. It's not up to you to be so bloody judgemental.'

'OK. So you don't understand how I feel. Fine.'

'You are acting like a four-year-old. And if you are wondering where Ted is, he's in Paris. He went to see you with a huge bunch of flowers to check you were OK. He booked tickets to a matinee and wanted to take you out to dinner. But – hey – don't worry about him. You just carry on worrying about yourself.'

'He's in Paris?'

'Yep.'

'Oh Christ.'

Charlie turned away. She hated being nasty to her closest friend, but Mary needed a bit of a shake.'

. . .

WE'LL ALWAYS HAVE PARIS

Rosie and Derek sat across from one another at the small café in their hotel's reception. The clinking of cups and muted conversations around them seemed jarringly normal compared to the storm brewing between them.

Rosie's fingers tapped an agitated rhythm on the tabletop, her gaze fixed on the untouched espresso before her. Derek cleared his throat, his hands wrapped tightly around his cup as if it could anchor him to the moment.

'Rosie, I—' Derek began, his voice low and strained.

'Don't.' Rosie's eyes snapped up to meet his, blazing with a mixture of hurt and anger. 'Just don't, Derek. I know you told our daughter we were splitting up and let her believe it was my fault. How could you?'

Derek's shoulders sagged. He ran a hand through his greying hair, a gesture so familiar it made Rosie's heart ache despite herself.

'I didn't mean to,' he said, his words tumbling out. 'I just... I couldn't bear to see the disappointment in her eyes. I was a coward, Rosie. I know that now.'

Rosie's laugh was sharp and brittle. 'A coward? That's putting it mildly. Do you have any idea what you've done? Mary won't even speak to me. She's fled Paris, Derek. Our holiday is ruined, our family is in tatters, and it's all because you couldn't be honest.'

Derek winced at each accusation as if they were physical blows. 'I know, I know. I've made a mess of everything. I'm so sorry, Rosie. I never meant for it to happen like this. I'm finding it all so hard…'

'You're finding it hard?' Rosie interrupted, her voice rising slightly before she caught herself, glancing around at the other patrons. She leaned in, her words fierce and low. 'You're the one who's dumping me, Derek. Imagine how I feel.'

Derek's face crumpled. 'I never wanted to hurt you, or

Mary. I just... I don't know how we got here, Rosie. How did we drift so far apart?'

Rosie's eyes glistened with unshed tears. 'We didn't drift, Derek. You steered us onto the rocks when you decided to have an affair.'

Derek flinched at the word. 'I know. I've made terrible mistakes. But please, Rosie, you have to believe me when I say I never intended for any of this to happen.'

'Intentions don't count for much right now,' Rosie said, her voice thick with emotion. 'What matters is what you're going to do to fix it. Mary needs to know the truth, and it needs to come from you.'

Derek nodded slowly, his face a mask of misery. 'You're right. I'll call her, explain everything. I'll make this right, Rosie. Somehow.'

Rosie stood, her chair scraping against the floor. 'I hope you can, Derek. For all our sakes.' She paused, looking down at the man she had loved for so long, now a stranger to her.

As Rosie walked away, her back straight and head held high, Derek watched her go. The weight of his actions settled over him like a shroud, leaving him alone at the table, surrounded by the cheerful chatter of strangers, feeling more lost than he ever had.

MARY'S FINGERS trembled as she dialled Ted's number. The phone rang three times before his familiar voice answered, tinged with worry.

'Mary? Where are you? I've been trying to reach you for hours.'

She closed her eyes, picturing Ted in their favourite Parisian café, probably still clutching the roses he'd mentioned in his last text. 'Ted, I'm so sorry. I'm at home. I... I had to get away.'

WE'LL ALWAYS HAVE PARIS

A pause. Then, softly, 'What happened?'

Mary's voice caught. 'Everything's falling apart. Dad... he's been having an affair. He's leaving Mum, not the other way around. I couldn't stay there, couldn't face them.'

'Oh, Mary.' Ted's sympathy washed over her, making her eyes sting with fresh tears.

'I'm so sorry. I know you went all that way. The lunch, the matinee... I've ruined everything.'

'Hey, none of that matters now,' Ted assured her. 'I'm just worried about you. Are you okay?'

Mary's laugh was watery. 'Not really. I've been horrible to Mum, Ted. I said such awful things and all this time...'

'It's not your fault. You didn't know.'

Mary's gaze fell on her hastily packed suitcase. 'I'll come back. I'll get on the next train to Paris.'

'I'd love that,' said Ted. 'I'll phone up and buy your ticket; my treat.'

Mary sank onto the bed, clutching the phone like a lifeline. 'What would I do without you?'

'Let's hope you never have to find out,' Ted said, his smile evident in his voice. 'Now, tell me about Hampton Court. Is it as beautiful as they say?'

Mary laughed as she described the pretty place they both knew so well: their home. She felt the knot in her chest loosen slightly. The world was still in chaos, but Ted's steady presence on the other end of the line anchored her, reminding her that not everything had to fall apart at once.

CHAPTER 20: RETURN TO PARIS

The Eurostar glided into Gare du Nord, its sleek body coming to a halt with a gentle hiss. Mary stepped onto the platform, eyes scanning the crowd until they landed on Ted. He stood there, a bouquet of slightly wilted roses still clutched in his hand, a patient smile on his face.

Mary's pace quickened, her luggage forgotten as she crashed into Ted's embrace. The roses were crushed between them, their sweet scent mingling with the salt of Mary's sudden tears.

'I'm so sorry,' she mumbled into his shirt. 'I've been so selfish.'

Ted's arms tightened around her, one hand stroking her hair. 'Shh, it's okay. You're here now.'

They stood like that for a moment, an island of stillness in the bustling station. Finally, Mary pulled back, wiping her eyes. 'I've ruined your flowers.'

Ted glanced at the crumpled bouquet and chuckled. 'They've had a long day. I think they'll forgive us.'

As they collected Mary's luggage, Ted's hand found hers,

their fingers intertwining with practised ease. 'Want to talk about it?' he asked gently.

Mary's lower lip trembled. 'It just hurts so much, Ted. I keep thinking about our family holidays, the dinners, the laughter. Was it all fake? Were they miserable the whole time?'

Ted guided them to a quiet corner of the station. 'Mary, look at me,' he said, his voice soft but firm. 'Would you prefer your parents stayed in an unhappy marriage?'

'No, of course not, but...'

'No buts,' Ted interrupted, his thumb caressing her knuckles. 'Your childhood wasn't a lie. People change, feelings change, but that doesn't negate the good times you had.'

Mary leaned into him, drawing strength from his steady presence. 'I feel like such a child, running away like that.'

'You were hurt and confused,' Ted reasoned. 'But now it's time to face this head-on. You're not a child anymore, love. You're a strong, incredible woman who can handle this.'

A ghost of a smile touched Mary's lips. 'When did you get so wise?'

Ted grinned, lifting their joined hands to kiss her fingers. 'I married up. Now, what do you say we arrange dinner with your parents? You have questions, and they deserve a chance to answer them.'

Mary nodded, her resolve strengthening. 'You're right. But first...' She pulled him closer, her eyes twinkling mischievously. 'I believe I promised to show you the sights in my bedroom.'

Ted laughed, the warm sound washing over Mary like a balm. 'I thought you'd never ask. Let's see if we can get your old room back.'

As they made their way out of the station, Mary felt a weight lift from her shoulders.

. . .

Mary paused outside the restaurant and peered through the window. She could see her parents, their faces etched with worry. Her mother's slender fingers fidgeted with a napkin while her father's eyes darted anxiously around the room.

Taking a deep breath, Mary pushed open the door. The soft bell tinkling announced her arrival, and her parents' heads snapped up in unison. Their faces transformed instantly – relief, joy, and love washing over their features.

Rosie stood first, her arms outstretched. 'Mary, darling,' she breathed, her voice catching.

Mary rushed into her mother's embrace, inhaling the familiar scent of Rosie's perfume. Derek joined them, his strong arms encircling them both.

'We're so glad you're here,' Derek murmured, his voice gruff with emotion.

As they separated, Mary noticed how her father's hand lingered on her mother's back and how Rosie leaned almost imperceptibly into his touch. The gesture spoke volumes about their history and connection, despite their current struggles.

They settled into their seats, an awkward silence falling over the table. Mary fidgeted with her menu, unsure where to begin.

Derek cleared his throat. 'Mary, we…'

'I'm sorry,' Mary blurted out, surprising herself. 'I shouldn't have run off like that. It was childish.'

Rosie reached across the table, squeezing Mary's hand. 'Oh, sweetheart. We're the ones who should be apologising. We handled this so badly.'

Derek nodded, his eyes filled with regret. 'We never meant to hurt you, pumpkin. Your mother and I, we...' He trailed off, glancing at Rosie.

In that moment, Mary saw something pass between her parents – a flicker of understanding, shared history, and love that hadn't quite died. It was subtle but unmistakable.

Rosie picked up where Derek left off, her voice gentle. 'We have a lot to explain, and we want to answer all your questions. But first, we need you to know that nothing – absolutely nothing – changes how much we love you.'

Mary felt tears prick her eyes. 'I know,' she whispered. 'I love you both too.'

Mary knew the conversation ahead wouldn't be easy, but looking at her parents – their relieved smiles, their tentative hope – she knew they would find a way through this together.

CHAPTER 21: THE PARISIAN PEACE TREATY

'Êtes-vous prêts à commander?' asked the waiter.

Derek, ever the diplomat, turned to Mary. 'Would you like to order first, pumpkin?'

Mary nodded, scanning the menu once more. 'Je voudrais le canard à l'orange, s'il vous plaît,' she said, her French flowing more smoothly than she'd expected.

'Excellent choice,' the waiter nodded approvingly. He turned to Rosie, who ordered the coq au vin, while Derek settled on the beef bourguignon.

'Did Ted not want to come?' asked Rosie. 'We were surprised not to see him when he arrived.'

'I think he wanted to give you space, so he checked into his room and had a little wander around.'

'And looked for you.'

'Well, yes, he probably spent much of the day wondering where I was.'

'It seems a shame that he hasn't come out tonight. Is he in the room on his own?'

'No, I left him in a restaurant about half a mile away. He thinks it's important for us to talk, and he said he'd meet us afterwards for a drink if we're up for it.'

'That would be nice,' said Rosie with a smile. Mary studied her parents, noticing the little details she'd overlooked before. The way her father smiled 'as soon as her mother did, almost mirroring her happiness. The way his eyes crinkled at the corners when he smiled, the soft curve of her mother's lips as she caught Derek's gaze.

'So, how are things? Are you enjoying Paris?'

Rosie's face lit up. 'Oh, it's as magical as ever. We took a stroll along the Seine, didn't we, Derek? The light at sunset was just breathtaking.'

Derek nodded, a wistful smile playing on his lips. 'Your mother insisted we stop at every bridge to take photos. We have about a hundred shots of the Eiffel Tower now.'

Mary laughed. 'Some things never change, do they? Remember our family trip when I was twelve? Mum made us pose for photos at every landmark.'

'Oh God,' Rosie groaned, but her eyes twinkled with amusement. 'Those hideous matching berets we bought...'

The three of them dissolved into laughter, the tension hanging over them dissipating slightly.

As their laughter subsided, the waiter returned with their appetisers. Mary inhaled deeply as her French onion soup was placed before her, the rich aroma of caramelised onions and melted cheese filling her senses.

'This smells divine,' she murmured, dipping her spoon into the golden broth.

Derek nodded in agreement, his eyes closing in appreciation as he tasted his escargots. 'I'd forgotten how good the food is here. Nothing quite compares, does it?'

Rosie hummed in agreement, delicately cutting into her goat cheese salad. 'We should come back more often, shouldn't we? As a family, I mean.'

A moment of awkward silence followed her words, the reality of their situation creeping back in.

Mary cleared her throat. 'So, um, about the... situation. When did you decide to split up? How long have you been considering it?'

Derek set down his fork, his expression turning serious. 'It wasn't an easy decision, Mary. Your mother and I have been drifting apart for a while now.'

Rosie's eyes met Derek's across the table. 'We still care for each other deeply, but...'

'But sometimes love changes,' Derek finished for her. 'We've realised we want different things out of life now.'

Mary stirred her soup absently, processing their words. 'I guess I just don't understand. You seem so... close. Even now.'

Rosie reached out, squeezing Mary's hand. 'Darling, just because we're separating doesn't mean we've stopped caring for each other. We've shared a life for over three decades. That doesn't just disappear overnight.'

Derek nodded. 'Your mother will always be one of the most important people in my life. And you, of course. This change doesn't affect how much we love you.'

Mary felt tears prick at her eyes. 'I know that, logically. It's just... hard to wrap my head around.'

The waiter arrived with their main courses, providing a welcome distraction. The rich aromas of perfectly cooked duck, tender chicken, and savoury beef filled the air.

As they began to eat, the conversation naturally drifted to lighter topics. They discussed Mary's work, Derek's latest bird-watching hobby, and Rosie's plans to redecorate the living room.

'You should see the colour swatches your mother's been looking at,' Derek chuckled. 'I think she's considering every shade of blue known to mankind.'

Rosie playfully swatted his arm. 'Oh, hush. It's an important decision. The living room sets the tone for the whole house.'

Mary watched their easy banter, a bittersweet feeling settling in her chest. How could two people who interacted so naturally, so lovingly, be ending their marriage?

As if reading her thoughts, Rosie turned to Mary. 'I know this must seem confusing, love. But sometimes, people can care for each other deeply and still realise they're better off apart.'

Derek nodded. 'We've had a wonderful life together and always cherish that. But we both deserve the chance to find happiness on our terms now.'

Mary took a sip of her wine, letting their words sink in. 'I suppose I understand that. It's just... what is the real story? Dad, you said that mum wanted the split, but then mum said that Dad was having an affair. Is there someone else, Dad? Because that's shitty if there is.'

Derek looked down at the table, clearly ashamed. 'There is someone else, Mary, yes.'

'So, how does that fit into all that bollocks you just spouted? What about 'sometimes, people can care for each other deeply' - you obviously don't care that deeply for Mum.'

Mary didn't want it to be an antagonistic dinner, but she had to ask the questions, and if her Dad was being a jerk to her Mum, she had to tell him straight.'

'I can see how upsetting this must all seem, Mary. I'm not a 20-year-old - I'm not jumping into bed with lots of different women; I've just met someone who makes me happy.'

'I bet she's not half the woman mum is.'

'Your mother is incredible, Mary. We're all lucky to have her in our lives.'

'So, what will it look like, moving forward? Will we still

have family dinners? Holidays?'

'Of course we will,' Rosie assured her. 'We're still a family, Mary. That hasn't changed.'

Derek reached across the table, squeezing Mary's hand. 'We'll figure it out together, pumpkin. It might be different, but it doesn't have to be bad. We can still have family dinners if that's what you want.'

'And you won't bring this old tart you've been seeing.'

'It'll just be the family,' said Derek.

As they finished their main courses, the conversation returned to Paris. They reminisced about the last time they had come to the city as a family decades ago. They laughed over long-forgotten mishaps and cherished memories.

'Remember when we got lost trying to find the Louvre?' Mary giggled. 'Dad was so sure he knew a shortcut...'

Derek groaned good-naturedly. 'In my defence, all these streets look the same after a while.'

Rosie shook her head, smiling. 'We ended up having the most wonderful picnic in that little park we stumbled upon. Sometimes getting lost leads you to the best discoveries.'

As the waiter cleared their plates, Mary felt a sense of peace. Yes, things were changing, but their love and warmth remained.

'Dessert?' Derek suggested, eyeing the menu. 'I hear the crème brûlée here is to die for.'

Rosie and Mary exchanged glances, both knowing Derek's sweet tooth all too well.

'Why not?' Mary smiled. 'We are in Paris, after all.'

The crème brûlée arrived, its caramelized top glistening in the soft restaurant lighting. Mary felt a surge of gratitude as they cracked into the desserts, savouring the rich, creamy sweetness.

'I just want you both to know,' she said, her voice thick with emotion, 'that I love you. And I'm here for you, whatever happens next. I'm not thrilled that you've met someone else, Dad, and I don't want anything to do with her - but I understand you are both making the best of this.'

Rosie and Derek reached out, each taking one of Mary's hands. In that moment, surrounded by the bustle of the Parisian restaurant, the three of them formed a circle of love and understanding that no change could break.

As they finished their desserts and prepared to leave, Mary felt a sense of optimism she hadn't expected when she'd first sat down. Yes, things were changing, but the core of their family – the love, the memories, the connection – remained unshakeable.

Stepping into the cool Parisian night, Mary linked arms with her parents. 'Fancy a walk along the Seine?' she suggested. 'For old times' sake? We could even pick Ted up on the way. '

Rosie and Derek exchanged a glance, then nodded in unison. 'Lead the way, pumpkin,' Derek smiled.

THE PARISIAN NIGHT air was cool against Rosie's skin as she stepped out onto the balcony of her hotel room later that night. The city's lights twinkled below. She picked up her phone and dialled her sister's number.

'Sue? It's me,' Rosie said, her voice wavering slightly.

'Rosie! How did it go?' Sue's concern was palpable even through the phone.

Rosie sighed, a mix of emotions colouring her voice. 'It was... lovely. We had a wonderful meal, and we seemed closer than ever. I can't help but wonder... do you think there's a chance we might get back together?'

On the other end of the line, Sue's stomach twisted. She knew things Rosie didn't, a burden she'd been carrying for days. 'Oh, Rosie,' she said softly, 'I wouldn't... I wouldn't hope for too much. These situations are complicated.'

Rosie's face fell, but she forced a cheerful tone. 'You're right, of course. I'm just being silly. Anyway, I'm looking forward to seeing you in the morning.'

Sue put down the phone and began chewing her nails, a nervous habit she thought she'd kicked years ago.

'Mark?' she called out to her husband. 'I need to talk to you.'

Mark appeared in the doorway, concern etched on his face. 'What's wrong, love?'

Sue's voice was low, urgent. 'It's about Derek. I know exactly who he's having an affair with, and Rosie... oh God, Rosie will hit the roof when she finds out.'

CHAPTER 22: THE REVELATION

Sunday

The next morning, Sue headed for Paris, her mind racing with the weight of her knowledge. As the train arrived at Gare du Nord, she steeled herself for the difficult conversations ahead.

Rosie was waiting for her sister, her face a mixture of relief and anxiety. The women embraced tightly, years of shared experiences and unspoken understanding flowing between them.

'Oh, Sue,' Rosie whispered, 'I'm so glad you're here.'

They made their way to a nearby café, the bustle of the station fading into the background. As they settled into their seats, Rosie began to speak, her words tumbling out in a rush.

'I suppose, at the end of the day, a marriage doesn't break up because one person is fed up. It's probably both our faults.'

Sue's head snapped up, her eyes wide with disbelief. 'Probably what? Have you had leave of your senses? None of this is your fault. It's all, completely, and utterly his fault. You sound like one of those women whose husband beats them but announces that it's probably their fault they were beaten.'

Rosie cringed at the comparison. 'You can't compare a marriage breaking up to someone being hit by their husband.'

'Yes, I can,' Sue insisted, her voice rising. 'That's exactly what I can compare it with. The misery and heartbreak that man has caused you is worse than any domestic violence incident. His behaviour is reprehensible, and I don't know why you're not taking him to the cleaners. You should have a solicitor lined up and scream for every penny he has. He is despicable.'

Rosie reached across the table, grasping her sister's hand. 'I admire your support,' she said softly, 'but it's not going to help me, and it's certainly not going to help Mary if I alienate Derek and have nothing to do with him. He's been very kind. He said that I can keep the house and—'

'Whoa, whoa, whoa. Hang on just there,' Sue interrupted, her voice sharp. 'What do you mean 'you can keep the house'? What does he think he's going to do, kick you out and move his fancy woman in?'

Rosie shook her head, her voice pleading. 'No, I'm just saying he is being reasonable, and so should I be. The best thing for me to do is not get so tied up in hate and revenge that I ruin my life. Derek and I will always be friends - you have to let me handle this in the way that's best for me.'

Sue's face softened slightly, but her eyes remained troubled. 'So you want me to just smile and be nice to him? Do you want me to talk politely to the man messing up my sister's life for no good reason? That's what you want?'

'That's what I want,' Rosie confirmed. 'I'd be very pleased if you would do that.'

Sue shook her head, barely containing her anger. It was all she could do to stop herself from charging up to Derek's room, smashing through it like the Incredible Hulk, and hurling him out of the window into the Seine. The idea of being civil to that little toad made her feel quite ill.

'Come on. we've got lots of fun things planned today. I've booked us into a rather fancy-looking Parisian Spa.'

'Oh, that sounds perfect. Just you, me and Mary?'

'I don't think Mary is coming. She said she didn't really fancy it.'

'She didn't fancy it? What? Mary loves that kind of thing. Is she OK?'

'I think so. She's quite thrown by all this stuff with Derek and me, though.'

'She's bound to be, love.'

'Yeah. She's hardly been drinking anything either, and you know what she's usually like.'

'She's a mad drunk, like you.'

'Well, I might not have put it like that, but - yes - we both like a drink.'

The sisters headed straight for the spa since Susan had no desire at all to drop her things off at the hotel and bump into Derek. She'd meet him tomorrow if she had to, but not yet.

As THEY LAY side by side, cucumber slices over their eyes and mud masks on their faces, Rosie continued to muse about her situation.

'You know, Sue,' she began, her voice dreamy, 'Derek's been so lovely through all of this. The way he looked at me during dinner... I can't help but wonder if maybe, just maybe, we might get back together. I had my suspicions that he'd met someone else, but I'm not sure now. He's been so lovely to me since we've been out here.'

Sue sat up abruptly, the cucumber slices flying off her

BERNICE BLOOM

face. 'DEREK'S HAVING AN AFFAIR WITH PAULINE!' she blurted out, unable to contain the secret any longer.

Rosie bolted upright, her mud mask cracking. 'PAULINE???' she gasped, her voice a mix of shock and betrayal. 'But she's my friend. I talk to her about the problems with Derek all the time. I thought we were close.'

Sue nodded grimly. 'She's only 50,' she added, her voice dripping with disdain.

'The bitch,' Rosie whispered. She felt as if her world was crumbling around her all over again. 'I really trusted her...'

ACROSS TOWN, Mary's phone buzzed with a message from her aunt Sue.

'Hey you. How are you? I need you to come to the spa. Your mum's very upset.'

'What's happened?'

'Love, can you come here so we can talk about it face-to-face?'

'Sure,' said Mary, packing a few things into her bag and saying goodbye to Ted.

'I thought you didn't want to go to the spa,' he said.

'Yeah, slight change of plan; Sue says mum's upset.'

'OK, you go and spa then. I might take your dad out for a beer.'

'Good plan,' said Mary, kissing her husband goodbye and rushing out of the room.

AT LE JARDIN DE SÉRÉNITÉ SPA, Rosie and Susan sat in lavender-scented splendour.

'Tell me everything,' Rosie whispered, her voice barely audible over the soft whale music designed to fill the clientele with peace and tranquillity.

Susan glanced around, ensuring their privacy before continuing. 'OK, well—to start with—Pauline has no idea that I know, and no one at the bridge club has any idea about this, so please don't think everyone is talking about you. No one knows.'

Rosie's felt a modicum of relief. 'Then how did you find out?'

Susan's face crumpled, words tumbling out. 'I saw them on Oak Street. Derek, he... he kissed her. At first, I thought maybe he was drunk, but...'

Rosie's vision blurred as hot tears spilt down her cheeks, smearing her carefully applied face mask. She barely registered the door opening, Mary's concerned voice cutting through her grief.

'Mom? What on earth happened?'

Susan guided Mary to a nearby chair, her eyes darting between the distraught Rosie and her concerned niece. 'Mary, I've just been talking to your mum. I know who Derek is having an affair with.'

Mary's brow furrowed as she took in her mother's state - Rosie's shoulders heaved with each sob, mascara and clay mask mingling in dark rivulets down her neck. 'What's going on? So, he's definitely having an affair? You are sure about this?'

'Yes. I saw him with another woman, kissing her. I'm so sorry, sweetheart. I wish it weren't true. But I saw them with my own eyes—your father and Pauline, on Oak Street.'

'Pauline?' Mary gasped, her mind reeling. 'Mom's friend Pauline? From bridge club?'

Susan nodded grimly. 'Yep.'

A hot flush of anger swept through Mary, her hands balling into fists at her sides. She glanced at her mother, who had curled into herself, face hidden behind trembling fingers. The sight only fueled Mary's rage.

'How long have you known?'

Susan winced. 'A few weeks. I wasn't sure what to do. I thought maybe it was a one-time thing, that he'd been drinking and made a mistake. But then I saw them again, and...' She trailed off, shaking her head.

Mary stood abruptly, nearly knocking over a small table laden with cucumber water and fresh fruit. 'I can't believe this,' she hissed. 'How could he do this to Mum? To our family?'

Mary began pacing the small lounge area, her mind racing. Then she had a thought. She pulled her phone from her purse.

'Don't ring her,' said Susan.

'I'm not,' said Mary. 'I'm texting Ted. He's with Dad right now.'

Her fingers flew across the screen as she composed a message:

'Ted, need your help. Found out Dad's cheating on Mum with Pauline. Mum's a mess. Find out what you can from Dad.'

She hit send, then turned back to her aunt and mother. Susan was now perched on the arm of Rosie's chair, rubbing soothing circles on her back. Mary knelt before her mother, gently prying Rosie's hands away from her face.

'Mum,' she said softly, her heart breaking at the sight of Rosie's red-rimmed eyes and tear-stained cheeks. 'Mum, I'm here. We're going to figure this out, okay?'

Rosie hiccupped, struggling to catch her breath. 'Oh, Mary,' she whimpered. 'How could he? After all these years...'

Mary felt her anger flare again but pushed it down, focusing on comforting her mother. 'I don't know, Mum. But we'll get to the bottom of this. I promise.'

As she held her mother close, Mary's phone buzzed with a reply from Ted: 'Holy shit. On it. Will call soon.'

. . .

'So, Derek,' Ted began, trying to sound casual, 'how long have you known Pauline from the bridge club?'

Derek raised an eyebrow. 'Pauline? Why do you ask?'

Ted's phone buzzed again. He glanced at it surreptitiously. 'Oh, just curious. And, uh, how often do you play bridge these days?'

As the afternoon wore on, Ted asked increasingly specific and personal questions, relaying the answers to Mary via text. Derek's confusion grew with each query.

'Ted, mate,' Derek finally said, eyeing him suspiciously, 'are you turning into a woman or something with all these questions?'

Back at the spa, the three women huddled together. Rosie's eyes were red-rimmed, causing the beautician to worry that the fask mask had caused her damage.

'Oh, Mum,' Mary said softly, pulling her mother into a tight embrace. 'I'm so sorry about all this.'

'I can't believe he dared to sit at dinner, playing happy families, when all along...'

Rosie's voice was small, broken. 'How could he? With Pauline, of all people?'

As the gravity of the situation settled over them, Mary's phone buzzed with another message from Ted. She read it aloud, her voice trembling slightly.

'Derek says he's sorry, that he never meant for any of this to happen, and that he still cares deeply for all of you. I don't get the impression that this fling wth Pauline will last. He's not got anything nice to say about her.'

Sue scoffed. 'Cares deeply? He has a funny way of

showing it. And it would serve Pauline right if this all blew up in her face.'

Rosie remained silent, her gaze fixed on some distant point. The weight of betrayal hung heavy in the air.

As the day wore on, the three women navigated a sea of emotions—anger, hurt, disbelief, and a tentative hope for the future. They laughed, cried, and raged against the unfairness of it all.

By evening, a sense of quiet resolution had settled over them. Rosie, her face tear-stained but determined, looked at her daughter and sister.

'Thank you,' she said softly. 'Both of you. I don't know what I'd do without you.'

Sue squeezed her hand. 'We're family. We stick together, no matter what.'

Mary nodded, her eyes shining with unshed tears. 'Always, Mum. Always.'

'I feel like I've lost a husband and a friend. It'll take some getting used to.'

'You haven't lost a friend. Friends don't treat each other like that. You've just found out what's she's really like.'

CHAPTER 23: SPA TIME

Rosie and Sue lounged in the spa's relaxation area, plush robes wrapped around them and glasses of infused water in hand. Mary had headed back to the hotel, leaving the two of them to listen to the soft, ambient music.

Rosie's gaze was fixed on her reflection in the large mirror across the room. She sighed, her voice barely above a whisper. 'I never thought I'd be in this position at my age. You know?'

Sue leaned in, her brow furrowed with concern. 'What do you mean?'

Rosie's fingers played with the belt of her robe. 'When you're younger, you don't know whether you'll keep a boyfriend for over a week. Even after we married, I never felt completely secure when other, more glamorous women were around.'

She paused, lost in memories. 'Especially when I was pregnant. You don't feel wonderful, and when you see the same man day in and day out, you stop making an effort. I'd see some of Derek's glamorous work colleagues and wonder if he wished I was more like them. But I never really thought for one minute that he would leave me. I thought he'd stay forever.'

Sue placed a gentle hand on her sister's shoulder, her touch conveying more comfort than words ever could.

Rosie continued, her voice growing stronger. 'But when you reach 60, you feel like you've done all the hard stuff. You're supposed to have a gentle couple of decades together, musing on the wonderful life you've created and your beautiful child. Making the most of your free bus pass, for heaven's sake! It's not the time of life for affairs.'

Sue nodded vigorously. 'Oh, Rosie, I completely agree with you. It's just heartbreaking, and I can't bear that he's done this to you.'

She hesitated, then asked, 'Do you think he really will move out and move in with her? Is there a chance he'll change his mind? He seemed so happy and settled here in Paris with the family around him. I just can't imagine him moving out.'

Rosie shook her head, her expression resolute. 'No, I think he's going. I don't think for a minute that he would put us all through this if he wasn't taking it very seriously.'

She let out a bitter laugh. 'To be honest, if he suddenly changed his mind now and wanted to stay, I'd be an absolute nutter to let him. How could I tell him to come back into our lives as if nothing had happened? I'd be forever wondering whether he was sneaking off with stupid, pathetic Pauline.'

Her voice rose slightly as she asked, 'What the hell has Pauline got?'

Sue's response was immediate and fierce. 'She's got nothing. Nothing at all. She's not attractive, she's not witty or clever, she's not warm and kind and lovely. She's not you. And she's not his wife. That's why I asked whether he would, in the end, actually go off with her. It seems bizarre that he would leave you and everything you've got and everything you've built for that mare.'

Rosie was baffled, as she had been from the start. The revelation that Derek was deciding to make a new life with Pauline was the most perplexing.

Pauline was more glamorous and outgoing than Rosie, but Rosie was more outgoing than Derek. She never imagined Derek wanting to go off with someone like her.

Pauline dressed well. Was that it? Rosie remembered those chocolate brown boots and thought they were nice.

Sue's voice broke through Rosie's reverie. 'Perhaps you should ask Mary to ask Ted what's so special about Pauline. He could ask Derek.'

Rosie shook her head firmly. 'No, I'm not going to do that. I'm going to try and be grown up about it. Mary's been through so much already. It's unfair to appear to pit ourselves against one another through Mary. I'll just try to forget and concentrate on myself.'

Rosie's first attempt at a spa treatment went slightly wrong when she cried so much that the face mask ran down her neck, but Sue insisted she try something else.

She handed Rosie a list of spa offerings, badly translated into English. Some of it was quite comedic, like those menus in restaurants that announce you will have 'penises in your soup' instead of peas. This treatment menu suggested 'electrifying shots' being directed at your skin.

Sue chuckled. 'I think they must mean a gentle electric current. I don't think electrifying your skin will do it any good.'

'Though, I know someone whose skin I would love to electrify,' Sue added, her tone half-joking, half-serious.

Rosie decided on a face contouring facial with 'electrifying impulses.' She lay on the bed and relaxed while the petite French aesthetician with very cold hands massaged her face, prodding and guiding her sharp knuckles under Rosie's cheekbones and jaw.

'For lifting,' said the woman. 'We lift.'

Rosie bit back a comment about how it was the skin sagging off the muscles that was the problem, and encouraging the muscles to lift probably wouldn't do a damn thing to prevent the sagginess.

As Rosie had predicted (and hoped), the' electrifying' was just a gentle electric current pushed into the skin through a metal device that stroked its way all over her face, making her muscles tingle and setting her teeth on edge.

She relaxed into a deep sleep, bizarre dreams of delivering carrots with Mary dancing through her subconscious. When the aesthetician gently woke her, Rosie felt relief wash over her.

'Thank God,' she murmured.

'You are OK?' the beautician asked, wiping some thick cream over Rosie's face.

'I'm fine. I was worried about delivering carrots, but it's all OK now.'

'Look, I show you your face.'

Rosie looked into the mirror and felt the shock everyone over 40 experiences when they see their mother looking back at them.

'You can see the jawline. Much better – yes?' the aesthetician asked hopefully.

'Oh yes, that's much better,' Rosie lied, not noticing a jot of difference between how her face looked now and how it looked before she came into the salon.

She walked out to see Susan sitting in reception, flicking through a French magazine she couldn't have understood.

'Oh wow,' said Susan, looking at her sister. 'You look amazing. That's made a real difference. Your skin is glowing.'

'Do you think so?' Rosie asked, doubt colouring her voice.

WE'LL ALWAYS HAVE PARIS

'When the beautician showed me in the mirror, all I could think of was how dreadful I looked without makeup.'

Sue's eyes softened. 'You look amazing. Then you've always looked amazing. I would hate you if you weren't my sister.'

'Come on, I'm going to buy you a glass of wine.'

As they went to the spa's bar, Rosie realised she hadn't complimented Sue on how she looked after her treatment.

'It's made your skin look years younger,' she said.

Sue burst out laughing. 'I didn't have a treatment in the end. I didn't fancy any of them.'

They both dissolved into giggles at the ridiculousness of it all. Did any of the treatments work? Who knew?

Settling into plush chairs with glasses of crisp white wine, the sisters reflected on the challenges of aging.

'You know,' Rosie mused, swirling the wine in her glass, 'getting older is like being on a rollercoaster you never asked to ride. One minute, you're feeling on top of the world; the next, you're plummeting down, wondering where all your youth went.'

Sue nodded, her eyes distant. 'Remember when we laughed at Mum for her 'senior moments'? Now I walk into a room and forget why I'm there half the time.'

They shared a rueful chuckle.

'And don't get me started on the physical changes,' Rosie continued. 'I swear, I look in the mirror sometimes and wonder who that stranger is staring back at me.'

'Oh God, yes,' Sue groaned. 'The other day, I caught sight of myself in a shop window and nearly had a heart attack. When did I start to look so... old?'

Rosie reached out and squeezed her sister's hand. 'We're not old, Sue. We're... seasoned.'

They burst into laughter again, the sound echoing through the tranquil spa.

As their mirth subsided, a comfortable silence fell between them. Rosie's thoughts drifted back to Derek and Pauline, a frown creasing her brow.

'You know what the worst part is?' she said quietly. 'It's not just the betrayal. It's the feeling that I'm somehow obsolete, like I've passed my expiration date.'

Sue's eyes flashed with anger. 'Don't you dare think that, Rosie. You are beautiful, inside and out. Derek's an idiot if he can't see that.'

Rosie smiled weakly. 'Thanks, sis. But sometimes I can't help but wonder... is this it? Is this all there is to look forward to? Watching your husband run off with a younger woman while you sit at home with your free bus pass?'

Sue leaned forward, her voice intense. 'Absolutely not. This is not the end, Rosie. It's a new beginning. You've got years ahead of you to do whatever you want and be whoever you want to be. Without Derek holding you back.'

Rosie blinked, surprised by her sister's vehemence. 'You believe that?'

'I do,' Sue said firmly. 'And so should you. Age is just a number, Rosie. It's what you do with your time that matters.'

As they finished their wine, a new resolve seemed to settle over Rosie. She sat up straighter, a glimmer of her old spark returning to her eyes.

'You're right,' she said. 'I've spent too long defining myself by my relationship with Derek. Maybe... maybe this is my chance to rediscover who I am.'

Sue beamed at her sister. 'That's the spirit! Now, how about we go cause some trouble in Paris? Show these young things how it's done?'

Rosie laughed, a genuine, carefree sound she hadn't produced in weeks. 'Lead the way, sis. Lead the way.'

Both sisters felt a renewed sense of possibility as they left the spa, arm in arm. Yes, getting older had its challenges. Yes, life had thrown them a curveball. But together, they would face whatever came next with grace, humour, and a healthy dose of sisterly mischief.

'Let's call Mary and get her back out,' said Rosie. 'The night's still young.'

CHAPTER 24: C'EST BRIGITTE MACRON

As twilight descended on Paris, Rosie, Sue, and Mary sat in a cosy wine bar, feeling mellow as the soft glow of candlelight danced across their faces, reflecting in their wine glasses.

Mary's eyes sparkled as she gazed out the window. 'Look at all the lights down the river!' she exclaimed, her voice filled with childlike wonder. She pressed her palms against the glass, her breath fogging it slightly. 'Doesn't it make you want to come and live in Paris for the rest of your life?'

Sue snorted, swirling her wine glass. 'Not really.'

'Don't be such a killjoy,' Rosie chided, her cheeks flushed from the wine and the convivial atmosphere. She leaned back in her chair, a contented smile on her lips. 'I'll move out here with you, Mary. I'll retire to Paris, take a French lover, and live a life of delicious debauchery: overindulging in food, wine, and plenty of mischief.'

An awkward silence fell over the table. Mary shifted uncomfortably in her seat while Sue raised an eyebrow. Rosie, however, maintained her smile, a defiant glint in her eye. Why shouldn't she talk about taking a lover? If Derek was running off with Pushy Pauline, she was entitled to as many paramours as she pleased.

'I think it's what Paris has done to me,' Rosie mused, breaking the silence. She raised her glass. 'One more bottle for the road?'

'Yes!' Sue agreed enthusiastically, her glass already empty.

Mary shook her head, her hand resting on her stomach. 'I'll stick to water, thanks.'

Rosie's brow furrowed with concern. 'Are you sure, love? It's not like you to pass up wine.'

'I know, Mum,' Mary replied, her voice soft. 'I think it's all this drama – it's made me feel a bit queasy. I just want to enjoy Paris with my lovely relatives. No more drama.'

As the evening wore on, the wine flowed freely for Rosie and Sue while Mary sipped her water, watching her mother and aunt with amused affection as they got increasingly drunk. When they finally stepped out onto the bustling Parisian street, Rosie and Sue broke into an off-key rendition of 'Joe Le Taxi' at the sight of a passing cab.

Mary shook her head, laughing. 'You two are like a couple of toddlers when you've had too much wine. What are we going to do with you?'

Rosie's eyes suddenly lit up. 'I know! We should buy Mary beautiful red lipstick like the Parisians wear. I wanted to get you one the other day but couldn't decide on the colour.'

Sue, now practically dancing on the sidewalk, her beige Clarks shoes sliding on the cobblestones, clapped her hands. 'Yes! Red lipstick! And a beret for me!'

The three women made their way through the Parisian streets, Sue doffing an imaginary hat at every attractive man they passed, while Rosie led them with surprising determination towards a Chanel boutique.

As they entered the shop, an air of sophistication enveloped them. Rosie straightened her posture and approached the counter. 'Bonjour,' she said, her accent more confident than accurate. 'Je voudrais un lipstick rouge.'

The shop assistant nodded and led them to the makeup counter, a veritable feast for the eyes with its colourful cosmetics and fragrances. As the assistant began to show them different shades of red, a hush fell over the store.

'Why have you stopped talking?' asked Sue, with a slight stagger to the side.

Mary looked up from the mirror, where she was trying on a vibrant cherry red, to see a striking older woman entering the boutique. Dressed impeccably in head-to-toe Chanel, her blonde bob immaculate, she exuded an aura of elegance and power.

'It is Brigitte Macron,' the assistant whispered reverently. 'The First Lady of France.'

Macron walked through the shop and passed Mary, Rosie and Sue. Mary suddenly felt self-conscious about her scruffy clothes. The First Lady, however, greeted them warmly.

"Hello, ladies," Madame Macron said in perfect English, her eyes sweeping over the group as she passed. She paused mid-step, her gaze lingering on Rosie's tear-stained cheeks. "Is everything alright?"

Rosie blinked rapidly, trying to compose herself. Her fingers fumbled with a tissue from her purse, dabbing at her eyes. "Oh, it's nothing. We're just..."

Mary placed a comforting hand on her mother's shoulder. "We're having a bit of a difficult day, Madame."

The First Lady's brow furrowed with concern. She stepped closer, her voice lowering. "Perhaps I can help? Is there something you need?"

Rosie's lower lip trembled. The wine from lunch, the emotional weight of the past few weeks, and the unexpected kindness from this elegant stranger suddenly proved too much. "It's my husband," she blurted out, her words tumbling over each other. "He's left me. For someone younger. And tomorrow's my 60th birthday, and I just..." She gestured helplessly, fresh tears spilling down her cheeks.

Madame Macron's eyes softened with understanding. She reached out, gently squeezing Rosie's arm. "Oh, ma chère. Come, let's sit for a moment."

She glanced around, spotting a quiet corner of the boutique with a small seating area. "We'll find you the perfect lipstick after we talk, oui? Sometimes, a little colour can lift our spirits when we need it most."

As she guided Rosie towards the seats, Mary and her aunt exchanged stunned glances. What had begun as a simple shopping trip had rapidly become more extraordinary.

"What about your husband, chérie?"

Rosie's shoulders sagged. "He's leaving me. For a younger woman. Said he wanted to 'rediscover himself.'" She let out a bitter laugh that sounded more like a sob.

A mix of compassion and indignation flashed across the First Lady's features. She gently took Rosie's hand in hers. "Oh, ma pauvre. How long were you married?"

"Thirty-five years," Rosie whispered, a tear escaping down her cheek.

Madame Macron's grip tightened, her voice low and fierce. "Thirty-five years, and he throws it away like this? C'est scandaleux!"

The Parisian shop assistants exchanged astonished glances, clearly unused to seeing their First Lady engaged in such an intimate conversation with a tipsy English tourist.

"Listen to me. His choices do not define you. You are a woman of strength, of wisdom. Your worth does not diminish with age."

Rosie nodded, wiping her eyes. "I know, I know. It's just... I feel so lost. Like I'm suddenly invisible."

"Invisible?" Madame Macron's eyes flashed. "Non, non.

We will not allow this. You are vibrant; you are alive." She paused, a determined look settling on her face. "This birthday of yours will not be a day of mourning. It will be a celebration of you, of your new beginning."

Mary and her aunt watched in amazement as the First Lady of France continued to console and uplift Rosie, their conversation flowing from shared experiences to quiet laughter. It was as if the rest of the world had faded away, leaving these two women connecting over the universal experiences of love, loss, and resilience.

After what seemed like both an eternity and no time at all, Madame Macron stood, still holding Rosie's hand. "Come with me," she said, her voice warm but brooking no argument. "We are going to find you the perfect shade of lipstick. Something bold, something that says 'I am here, and I am magnificent'."

As they stood admiring their reflections after trying on the different lipsticks, a discreet cough interrupted them. A stern-looking man in a dark suit had appeared at Madame Macron's elbow.

"Madame," he murmured, "we must be going. The President is waiting."

Brigitte sighed dramatically. "Duty calls, I'm afraid. But before I go..." She scribbled something on a piece of paper and pressed it into Rosie's hand. "This is the address of a wonderful little restaurant. Tell them Brigitte sent you. They'll take good care of you."

With a final warm smile and a wave, the First Lady of France swept out of the boutique, leaving behind three shell-shocked women and the lingering scent of Chanel No. 5.

CHAPTER 25: BACK TO THE LOUVRE

'That was the weirdest moment of my life,' said Rosie as the three women left the shop and walked towards the Metro.

'Crazy,' said Susan. 'That was properly crazy.'

As the women waited to cross the road, a large black car purred to a stop next to them.

'Come in, have a lift,' said the man in the front passenger seat.

'No, thank you. We're fine,' said Mary.

'Madam Macron insists she would like you to accompany her,' said the man. 'Please get in.'

The women looked at one another before Mary opened the back door. 'Let me just check first,' she said. 'We're not getting in here until I know it's really her.'

She swung open the back door to be greeted by their old friend - Brigitte.

'Please. Come with me tonight. I am going to a drinks evening. . Let me invite you as a birthday treat.'

Rosie looked at Mary, and Mary looked at Sue. Sue looked from Mary's face to Rosie's face before jumping in the back of the car. 'Come on girls, it's not often you get asked out by the President's wife. Shift up so we can all get in.'

The car eased through the traffic, guided by police outriders until it pulled up in front of the Louvre. Madame Macron stepped out gracefully, turning to face Rosie, Sue, and Mary with an inviting smile.

'Do come,' she said.

Sue's eyes widened with excitement, and she practically bounced on her toes. 'Yes, of course!' she exclaimed.

Rosie hesitated, her brow furrowed with concern. 'We're at The Louvre,' she said to Mary. 'Is this a good idea? The last time we were here, we were thrown out and marched to a solicitor's office.'

Mary looked around. 'Mum, we're with the First Lady of France. There's no way we're getting chucked out. Besides, it was their fault for leaving the doors unlocked.'

Rosie's frown deepened. 'I don't want us to end up in a French jail overnight.'

Before Mary could respond, Madame Macron's melodious voice floated back to them. 'The Louvre is a very special place. So much French history, such a beautiful gallery. You will adore it.'

As they approached the grand entrance, the air buzzed with anticipation. Flashes of light exploded around them as photographers clamoured for the perfect shot. Mary felt a moment of self-consciousness as she stepped onto the red carpet, suddenly aware of her crumpled clothing and scruffy trainers amidst the sea of designer gowns and sparkling jewels.

Madame Macron, sensing their unease, touched Rosie's hand gently. 'Please don't worry. Everyone is very nice here. They will be delighted to see you.'

As they entered the grand hall, Mary's breath caught in her throat. The Louvre, already magnificent by day, was transformed into a fairytale wonderland. Tiny lights twinkled like stars, casting a warm glow over the priceless artworks, their shimmer reflecting off the polished floors.

Suddenly, a familiar voice cut through the elegant murmur of the crowd. 'Hello Mary! How are you doing?'

Mary whirled around, her eyes searching for the source of the greeting. It took her a moment to realise that the voice came from one of the 'statues' placed around the room – her mime artist friend from earlier in the week.

'Oh my God. How are you? It's lovely to see you again,' said Mary.

'Is everything okay? Did you find your dad?' the mime artist asked, his painted face betraying a hint of genuine concern.

Mary grinned, gesturing to Rosie and Sue. 'Yes, thank you so much. This is my mum, and this is my auntie.'

The statue's eyebrows rose, disappearing beneath his metallic wig. 'You did well to get a place at the front. Isn't this supposed to be an elite gathering?'

Mary felt a flush of pride as she explained their chance encounter with Madame Macron. As she spoke, she noticed several guests eyeing them curiously, no doubt wondering about the oddly-dressed trio in their midst.

As the evening wore on, Mary found herself caught between two worlds – the glittering, high-society event swirling around her and the awkwardness and pain emanating from her mother. She watched as her mother sipped champagne nervously while Aunt Sue seemed determined to try every hors d'oeuvre that passed by.

Just as Mary was beginning to relax, she caught sight of a familiar face – the security guard who had escorted them out earlier that day. His eyes narrowed as he approached, recognition dawning on his face.

'Do I know you from somewhere?' he asked, his tone suspicious.

Mary's heart raced, but she managed a calm smile. 'I'm a friend of Madame Macron,' she said, silently praying he wouldn't press further.

The guard's eyes lingered on her momentarily before he nodded slowly. 'That's fine. Just don't go through doors or mess with anything that's not your business.'

As he walked away, Mary let out a breath she didn't realise she'd been holding. She turned to her mother and aunt, suddenly feeling the weight of the day's adventures.

'How much more of this do we have to do?' she asked, stifling a yawn.

Rosie looked at her daughter with amusement. 'You seem to be tired all the time. There's supposed to be a performance in the main room. Shall we have a look? Then we can head off if you want.'

As they made their way through the crowded galleries, Mary marvelled at the surreal turn their evening had taken. From a simple lipstick purchase to rubbing elbows with the elite of Paris – all while trying to avoid detection from the security team that had thrown them out days earlier.

By the time they finally stepped out of the Louvre, Mary was exhausted. It was as if exhaustion was settling into her bones. Why was she so tired all the time?

CHAPTER 26: AN ANNOUNCEMENT

Monday

The elegant Parisian restaurant bustled with quiet conversation and the soft clink of fine china. Rosie sat at the head of the table, her 60th birthday celebration in full swing. The warm glow of candlelight softened the lines on her face, making her look years younger. Her eyes, though, held a mixture of joy and melancholy that betrayed the complexity of her emotions.

Derek sat to her right, his fingers fidgeting with his napkin. Every so often, his gaze would drift to Rosie, a look of guilt and longing flashing across his face before he quickly averted his eyes. Susan, seated across from him, didn't miss these furtive glances. Her lips were pressed into a thin line, barely containing her simmering anger.

'I bet you didn't expect to be here with your husband about to run off with another woman,' Susan said, her voice dripping with disdain as she glared at Derek.

Rosie sighed, reaching out to pat her sister's hand. 'Not tonight, Susan. Let's just celebrate my 60th.'

Derek looked at his wife, her grace and reasonableness

hitting him like a physical blow. A pang of guilt, followed quickly by a surge of love, washed over him. He found himself wishing he'd never met Pauline, never accepted that fateful glass of wine, never glimpsed those stocking tops as she crossed her legs. But it was too late now. He was in love with Pauline.

Or was he? Could a man love two women at the same time? The love he felt for Rosie was different - she was his anchor, his reason for being. But they hadn't been intimate for years, not since Rosie hurt her back and started sleeping in another bed. With Pauline, he felt young again, alive in a way he hadn't for decades. Was it selfish to want that spark, that excitement?

As the main course arrived, Mary's eyes kept darting to the restaurant's entrance. Ted was supposed to be sneaking in a birthday cake, but he was running late.

'Is that Ted?' Rosie asked, peering at a figure outside the restaurant window.

Mary's heart skipped a beat. 'Probably not,' she said quickly. 'He can't make it. He's got some work he's got to catch up on.'

Rosie's face fell slightly. 'It's a shame he has to work on my birthday. Couldn't he have done it another time?'

Before Mary could respond, Ted burst through the kitchen doors, looking flustered and carrying a large box that seemed to have been punched on both sides.

Mary stared at him, her face a mix of amusement and exasperation. 'Yeah, a bit of an issue with the box,' he said. Mary shook her head fondly. 'You're more like me every day,' she said, barely containing her laughter.

The meal progressed - a strange mix of delicious food and tense undercurrents. Aunty Susan couldn't resist taking jabs at Derek, at one point declaring that her fried fish 'has all the beauty of Pauline.'

Rosie was determined not to let talk of Pauline spoil the evening. She was heartbroken by what she'd discovered and furious with Derek for the betrayal, but she needed a break for one evening. Just a few hours of celebration without being reminded of the hurt and disappointment.

'You have to stop this, Susan,' Rosie pleaded, her voice tinged with exhaustion.

Susan stabbed her pudding with unnecessary force. 'Sure,' she muttered, her eyes never leaving Derek's face.

As the dessert plates were being cleared, Mary suddenly felt a wave of nausea. She took a deep breath, steadying herself. It was time.

'Mum,' she said, her voice trembling slightly. 'I have something to tell you.'

The table fell silent, all eyes turning to Mary. She reached for Ted's hand under the table, drawing strength from his reassuring squeeze.

'I'm pregnant.'

CHAPTER 27: THE AFTERMATH

'This is wonderful,' she said. 'You're pregnant, Mary. That's such lovely news. What, how, when? I need to know everything.'

Mary laughed, her cheeks flushed with excitement. 'Forgive me for not answering 'how', but I'm only just pregnant - about five weeks, we think. I was going to tell you in a few weeks, you know - after the eight-week mark, but it's great news - and great news is what we need right now, so I thought I'd tell you.'

The words hung in the air for a moment before the table erupted in a cacophony of exclamations and questions. Rosie's eyes filled with tears of joy as she embraced her daughter. Even Derek and Susan temporarily forgot their animosity, caught up in the excitement of the news.

As the commotion settled, Rosie looked around the table at her family - her estranged husband, her protective sister, her beloved daughter and son-in-law, and the promise of a new life on the way. Despite the challenges that lay ahead, in that moment, surrounded by love and the promise of new beginnings, Rosie felt truly blessed.

The waiter appeared, carrying a beautifully decorated birthday cake adorned with sparkling candles. As the restaurant broke into a chorus of 'Happy Birthday,' Rosie closed her eyes, made a wish, and blew out the candles. Whatever the future held, she knew she would face it with the strength and grace that had carried her through sixty remarkable years.

As the initial shock wore off, the questions began to flow.

'How have you been feeling?' Rosie asked, studying her daughter's face for any signs of morning sickness or fatigue.

Mary grinned. 'Honestly? I've stopped drinking, I get madly tired all the time, and I've been having the weirdest dreams, Mum. I mean, bonkers dreams. I dreamt last night that I was in a carpark, at the ticket machine, waiting to pay to leave.

'If you didn't want to pay, you could do a forfeit instead. The guy in front of me had the forfeit to wee all over my dog. The machine kept chanting, 'Wee on Elvis, then you can leave, wee on Elvis, and then you can leave.'

'That's properly odd. The machine was talking to you? What? Like a humanoid?'

'No, not a humanoid. Why would you say 'humanoid'?' replied Mary.

'Yeah, doesn't sound like a humanoid - there's no such thing,' said Rosie.

Ted shook his head. 'OK. Not a humanoid then. Whatever.'

'I have odd dreams all the time,' Mary said, trying to steer the conversation away from humanoids. 'That's why I wake up in a right panic some mornings.'

'Because you thought an old man was about to wee all over little Elvis?' Ted asked.

'Yes! So that he could get his parking for free!'

As the laughter subsided, a comfortable silence fell over

the table. Rosie found herself observing the interplay between Mary and Ted, the way they finished each other's sentences and shared secret smiles. It reminded her of the early days with Derek, and she felt a pang of nostalgia.

Derek, as if sensing her thoughts, caught her eye across the table. His expression was soft, tinged with regret and something else - hope, perhaps? Rosie quickly looked away, her heart beating a little faster.

'I want everything for my baby,' Mary said suddenly, her voice filled with determination. 'I want the best schools, the best care, everything. I want him to do really well... I mean - not like me, I was terrible at school, wasn't I?'

Rosie chuckled. 'It wasn't so much that you hardly ever went to school, more that you made guest appearances.'

Derek joined in, his voice warm with affection. 'Remember the time you decided to stage a protest against school uniforms by showing up in your pyjamas?'

Mary groaned, burying her face in her hands. 'Oh God, I'd forgotten about that. Didn't I end up in detention for a week?'

'Two weeks,' Rosie corrected, her eyes meeting Derek's over Mary's bowed head. They shared a smile, the kind that only parents who've weathered the storms of raising a spirited child can truly appreciate.

As the evening wore on, the conversation flowed freely, punctuated by laughter and moments of quiet reflection. Rosie found herself studying Derek when he wasn't looking, noticing the new lines around his eyes, the touch of grey at his temples. Despite everything, he was still the man she had fallen in love with all those years ago.

Derek, for his part, couldn't help but be struck by Rosie's grace and resilience. Here she was, celebrating her 60th birthday in the midst of personal turmoil, yet she radiated warmth and joy. He felt a twinge of guilt, wondering not for the first time if he was making a terrible mistake.

'Happy birthday, Rosie,' Derek said softly, raising his glass in a toast. The rest of the table followed suit, a chorus of well-wishes filling the air.

As Rosie blew out her candles, she made a silent promise to herself. Whatever the future held, whether it included Derek or not, she would face it with courage and grace. And who knew? Perhaps this birthday celebration was not just an ending but a new beginning.

The cake was cut and distributed, its rich chocolate flavour earning appreciative murmurs from around the table. As they savoured the dessert, the conversation turned once again to Mary's pregnancy.

'Have you thought about names yet?' Rosie asked, her fork poised halfway to her mouth.

Mary and Ted exchanged a glance. 'Well,' Mary began, a mischievous glint in her eye, 'we were thinking of Archibald if it's a boy and Ethel if it's a girl.'

The table fell silent momentarily before bursting into laughter at the horrified expressions on Rosie and Derek's faces.

'She's joking,' Ted assured them, gently patting Mary's hand. 'We haven't discussed names yet. It's still early days.'

As the laughter subsided, Derek leaned forward, his expression serious. 'You know, whatever you need - both of you - Rosie and I are here for you. This baby will be loved beyond measure.'

Rosie nodded in agreement, touched by Derek's words. For a moment, the spectre of their impending separation vanished, replaced by the shared excitement of becoming grandparents.

As the evening drew to a close, Rosie found herself reluctant to leave. This dinner had been more than just a birthday celebration; it had been a reminder of the strong bonds that held their family together, even in the face of adversity.

Standing outside the restaurant, waiting for taxis, Rosie shivered slightly in the cool night air. Without a word, Derek slipped off his jacket and draped it over her shoulders, his hands lingering for a moment longer than necessary.

'Thank you,' Rosie said softly, looking up at him. In the glow of the streetlights, she could see the conflict in his eyes, the struggle between what he thought he wanted and what he knew was right.

'Rosie, I-' Derek began but was cut off by the arrival of their taxi.

As they climbed into the back seat, Rosie wondered what Derek had been about to say. Was it possible that he was having second thoughts about leaving? But even if he was - could she possibly stay with him after all this?

The taxi wound its way through the lamp-lit streets of Paris, the city of love living up to its reputation with its romantic ambience. Rosie and Derek sat in companionable silence, each lost in their own thoughts.

As they neared their hotel, Derek's hand found Rosie's in the darkness of the backseat. He gave it a gentle squeeze, a gesture that spoke volumes without a single word being uttered.

Stepping out of the taxi, they lingered in front of the hotel entrance for a moment. The night was clear, the stars twinkling overhead like a blanket of diamonds.

'Do you fancy a nightcap?' asked Derek.

Rosie smiled. She thought about all the pain, all the tears, and all the anger he'd caused. Then thoughts of Pauline came into her mind.

'No thanks,' she said, shrugging off Derek's jacket and handing it back to him.

Derek nodded, his eyes never leaving her face. 'Rosie, I-'

he paused, struggling with his words. 'I just want you to know that, no matter what happens, you will always be one of the most important people in my life. The mother of my child, the grandmother of my grandchild. That will never change.'

'Good night, Derek,' she said, walking into the hotel alone, leaving him standing outside.

CHAPTER 28: AT THE END

It was Tuesday. The morning after the night before. Paris was painted in soft hues of pink and gold as the city slowly stirred to life.

Mary stood at her hotel window, watching the Seine glisten below, a gentle steamboat gliding under the bridges. The Eiffel Tower stood resplendent in the distance, a silent sentinel over the awakening city.

A gentle knock at the door broke her reverie. 'I wondered whether you might be up,' her mum asked. 'Do you fancy breakfast before we go to the station?'

Mary's heart swelled with a mix of emotions. 'I'd love that,' she said, reaching out to hug her. 'I'm sorry I didn't tell you sooner about the baby. I wanted to, but then with Dad and everything, it all became too difficult.'

'Don't be silly,' said Rosie, hugging her daughter. 'It was a lovely birthday surprise when you told me last night.'

As they made their way to a nearby café, the streets were just beginning to buzz with early risers. The aroma of freshly baked croissants and brewing coffee filled the air, mingling with the crisp morning breeze.

Settling into a quaint corner table, with a view of the street and the river beyond, they ordered a breakfast spread that would make any Parisian proud - buttery croissants, pain au chocolat, fresh fruit, and steaming cups of café au lait.

As they began to eat, Rosie cleared her throat. 'I've been doing a lot of thinking,' she began, her eyes watching Mary. 'This week... it's made me realize how important family is. How important you and Ted are to me.'

'I've felt the same with you, Mum. I'm so sorry about all the drama and rushing back home. I just couldn't cope.'

'I know sweetheart.'

'And I can't believe I blamed you.'

'I think that was your dad's fault.'

'Yes. All of this is dad's fault.'

'Don't be too hard on him.' said Rosie.

'Why? I think we should all be very hard on him.'

'There's no point. What's done is done. He'll be a great dad and a great grandpa. I'm still desperately hurt, but there's no point in fighting him or making things worse.'

'Gosh, mum. I wish I could be like you. I'd have stabbed him through the heart and cut Pauline into a million pieces by now. In fact, I still might. As soon as we get home.'

'Hello, hello. What's going on here?' came a voice.

Derek stood next to the table.

'Can I join you?'

Rosie and Mary exchanged a glance.

'Of course, you can, Dad,' said Mary.

Rosie smiled at her daughter.

'Look - there's something I need to say... I'm sorry.'

'Yes,' said Mary. 'I think we know that.'

She would try to be nice and not punch Pauline in the face, but she couldn't promise.

'I've decided to slow things down with Pauline. I was nuts to think we could move on so quickly.'

He turned to Rosie, his eyes full of regret and admiration. 'You're an amazing woman, Rosie.'

Rosie's hand trembled slightly as she reached for her coffee cup. 'Thank you, Derek,' she said, her voice barely above a whisper.

Mary watched her parents, a lump forming in her throat. The pain was still there, but so was hope - hope for a future where they could all coexist, if not as a traditional family, then as something new and equally valuable.

'I have so many questions,' Mary said, breaking the silence. 'When you told me you were splitting up, it felt like a part of me had been removed. I know I'm grown up and appreciate what Ted says - that you're entitled to live your own lives - but it still hurts. It makes me wonder whether you were ever truly happy, whether my childhood was all pretence.'

Rosie reached out, taking Mary's hand in hers. 'Oh, darling, no. Your childhood was real. The love we had for you - have for you - is real. And we were truly happy for a very long time.'

Derek nodded in agreement. 'Life is complicated, sweetheart. People change, and feelings evolve. But that doesn't negate our good times or the family we built.'

As they talked, the café around them filled with the morning crowd. The clatter of dishes and the hum of conversation provided a soothing backdrop to their intimate discussion.

'I know it's hard being a parent,' Mary mused, absently rubbing her stomach. 'And I'm sure I'll soon find out just how hard. You're humans, with all the frailties that humans have. I shouldn't be too harsh on you, but I think the way you have treated Mum is despicable.'

'I know.'

Rosie's eyes filled with tears. 'Can we talk about you now, Mary? You're going to be an amazing mother. And we'll be here for you every step of the way.'

'Thank you,' said Mary. 'I never doubted that for a minute.'

The sun had fully risen as they finished breakfast, bathing Paris in its warm glow.

'Shall we walk along the Seine before we head to the station?' Derek suggested.

They strolled along the riverbank, the water shimmering beside them. Couples walked hand in hand, groups gathered; the city pulsed with life.

They paused as they reached a bridge, looking out over the water. The Eiffel Tower stood proud in the distance, a symbol of Paris and all it represented—love, beauty, and resilience.

'You know, there couldn't be a lovelier place to receive news you don't want to hear. If I had to find out that you two are splitting up, I'm glad it was here in Paris.'

Rosie smiled, linking her arm through her daughter's. 'That's my girl. She always finds the silver lining.'

'That's me,' said Mary. 'I'm the silver-lining-hunter.'

The words hung in the air, full of meaning and promise. As they turned to make their way to the hotel, Mary felt a sense of peace settle over her. Yes, things were changing, but change didn't have to mean an end. It could be a beginning.

They collected their bags and met with Ted and Susan before beginning the journey home.

'You know,' Derek said suddenly, 'I was thinking about names for the baby.'

Ted raised an eyebrow. 'Oh? And what did you come up with?'

'Well,' he said, a mischievous glint in his eye, 'how about Seine for a girl? Or Eiffel for a boy?'

'We'll think about it,' said Mary.

Mary took one last look at Paris through the window as they sat on the train. The city of light had worked its magic, illuminating not just the streets and buildings but also the bonds between them. They were entering a new chapter, one filled with uncertainty but also with hope.

The train pulled out of the station, gathering speed as it left Paris behind. Mary sat still, her parents on either side of her and her husband and aunty opposite her. She knew that they carried a piece of Paris with them - not just in their memories, but in their hearts.

Mary closed her eyes as the French countryside began to blur past the windows, her hand resting protectively over her stomach. She thought of the weekend—the shock, the tears, the laughter, the revelations—and smiled.

They would always have Paris and each other.

WANT TO FIND OUT WHAT HAPPENS NEXT?
'She's Stolen My Baby' is the next book

CLICK BELOW FOR MORE INFORMATION
My Book

FIND OUT?
Will Mary cope with Motherhood?
Will Derek come rushing back to Rosie?
Will Mary hit Pauline? Will Susan hit Pauline?
And - who on earth is trying to steal Mary's baby

ALSO BY BERNICE BLOOM

The order of the Mary Brown books:

What's Up, Mary Brown? (The Mary Brown novels Book 1)

Link: My Book

The Adventures of Mary Brown (The Mary Brown novels Book 2)

Link: My Book

Christmas with Mary Brown: Fun, Joy & Laughter (The Mary Brown novels Book 3)

Link: My Book

Mary Brown is leaving town: Fun and laughter at weight loss camp & the joys of internet dating (The Mary Brown novels Book 4)

Link: My Book

Mary Brown in Lockdown (The Mary Brown novels Book 5)

Link: My Book

The Mysterious Invitation: A Mary Brown novel (The Mary Brown novels Book 6)

Link: My Book

A friend in need, Mary Brown: A NOVELLA (The Mary Brown novels Book 7)

Link: My Book

Dog Days for Mary Brown: A NOVELLA (The Mary Brown novels Book

Link: My Book

Don't Mention The Hen Weekend: A Mary Brown Novel (The Mary Brown novels Book 9)

Link: My Book

The St. Lucia Mystery (The Mary Brown novels Book 10) -

Link: My Book.

We'll Always Have Paris (out in August)

My Book

LINK: My Book.

All the books together:

https://www.amazon.co.uk/.../Bernice-Bloom/author/B01MPZ5SBA

Then...coming soon...

WANT TO READ MORE ABOUT ROSIE BROWN?

Three more books about Rosie are coming soon...

Sassy and Sixty, Golden Girls & Grans Just Wanna Have Fun

Get ready for a wild ride with Rosie Brown, the sassy sixty-year-old about to show the world that age is just a number.

Her mission to take control of her life begins when she gets out of bed and realises that every part of her is starting to creak. All she's done is lie down for eight hours, but she has the sort of neck pain that a younger person would associate with severe whiplash from a multi-car pile-up.

There are so many clicks and clacks from her creaking joints it sounds like someone's knitting next to her as she walks. Serenaded by knitting needles when she used to be serenaded by handsome young men. How on earth did this happen?

She catches her reflection and gasps - when did she start looking like her own grandmother? But hold onto your dentures, folks, because Rosie's not going down without a fight!

On the brink of divorce, disillusioned, and desperately eyeing those comfy Clarks shoes, Rosie decides it's time to dust off her leopard print and channel her inner twenty-something.

What follows is a hilarious journey of self-rediscovery that'll have you laughing, crying, and cheering from the sidelines.

Watch Rosie trade her sensible slacks for sassy stilettos as she shimmies through dance classes, leaving a trail of shocked faces and dropped jaws in her wake. Will her ex-husband Derek's eyes pop out of his head when he sees the new Rosie? You bet your bingo wings they will!

But the real fun begins when Rosie meets her new partners in crime - a gang of sixty-something troublemakers who prove that mischief has no age limit. From crashing singles mixers to staging senior citizen flash mobs, these golden girls are painting the town red... and maybe a few other colours they can't quite remember the names of.

Will Rosie find love again? Will she rediscover her zest for life? Or will she end up in a mobility scooter drag race down Main Street?

'Sassy and Sixty' is a heartwarming tale that proves it's never too late to rewrite your story - even if you need reading glasses to see the page.

So grab your most outrageous hat, pour yourself a cheeky glass of sherry, and get ready to join Rosie on the adventure of a lifetime!

Warning: This book may cause spontaneous laughter, uncontrollable urges to tango, and a sudden desire to dazzle your walking stick. Reader discretion is advised!

Printed in Great Britain
by Amazon